T0367889

# STOWAWAY

## *by Donald Christopherson*

authorHOUSE®

AuthorHouse™ LLC
1663 Liberty Drive
Bloomington, IN 47403
www.authorhouse.com
Phone: 1-800-839-8640

Published by AuthorHouse    07/09/2013

ISBN: 978-1-4817-6228-1 (sc)
ISBN: 978-1-4817-6227-4 (e)

Library of Congress Control Number: 2013910542

# Chapter 1

It was a fine clear night as usual on the California desert. Carl Johnson always appreciated the warm, clear nights and the billions of stars in the sky. He came from the rainy, overcast regions of the northwest. Carl Johnson had graduated from the University of Oregon with a degree in computer science. He was 5' 10" tall and had blue eyes and brown hair. Tonight he wore a corduroy jacket, tan wash pants, and penny loafers. Carl was very inquisitive but not particularly self assertive.

It was the month of August in 2125. Carl was heading north on Highway 395 on his way to a military base near Canyon City, where he was going to install some changes in the base computer program. Typically he went from Los Angeles to San Bernardino and then took Highway 15 to its junction with 395, but sometimes he went from San Bernardino to Barstow and then took Highway 58 to its junction with 395. He was just now catching up to a long, flat bed truck with a dark canvas lashed down tightly over its load. When he was about to pass the truck, the truck's turn signal started flashing. So Carl fell back and began wondering onto what road the truck could possibly be turning out here in the middle of nowhere, or was it just going to pull over so the driver could inspect something. Just then they came upon a single road leading off to the right and Carl recognized it as the road he had seen on previous trips that apparently led off to an air force installation about a mile from the highway. He recalled that on previous day trips through this region he had noticed a sign by the side of the road identifying the base as Ellsworth Air Force Facility and that he had seen what appeared to be a white radar dome and some other buildings about a mile back from the road.

After the truck had turned off, Carl resumed his normal speed and fell to day dreaming about the excellence of the night. He decided to stop his car up ahead and get out and gaze at the stars for a while. He had done that before on a lonely road out in the desert and was absolutely amazed by the enormous number of stars in the clear sky. There weren't any lights or towns along this stretch of the highway so Carl thought he would have just as fine a view from here as from that lonely road in the desert between Canyon City and the Air Force test range where he worked.

Carl spotted a nice wide spot on the shoulder up ahead and decided to stop there. Any passing motorist would just assume that he had stopped for a rest and would go by without stopping. After he got out of the car and started contemplating the sky, Carl vowed once more that he was going to get one of those star maps and try to memorize the key constellations so that he would know where things are in the sky. He had read that the Andromeda Galaxy appears as a sort of light smudge about the size of a postage stamp. That is, if you knew where to look for it.

Just then several fairly bright lights showed up in the sky in the direction of the air force base. Carl fixed his attention on them and counted five lights; they were bluish and reddish in color and were apparently on some aircraft approaching the base. The lights moved so slowly that Carl thought that it must be a helicopter. The craft approached the base and finally hovered over it. Presently it began to descend.

Carl opened the car door and reached for his binoculars in the glove compartment. He decided he was going to climb one of the little hills or rises in the area to get a better look at the proceedings over at the base. Of course he would have to watch out for the snakes in this region.

When Carl got to the top of a little rise and focused his binoculars on the base he was startled to discover that it wasn't a helicopter but a large spaceship that was sitting on the landing pad. Trucks were backing up to the craft and fork lifts were moving forward. Carl checked his watch for the time; it was just 9:45 pm. The fork lifts were moving boxes from the trucks into the spaceship. He focused his binoculars as best he could and strained hard to get a glimpse of the crew members of the spaceship. Everybody looked about the same size. There weren't any little green men. The people loading the spaceship all had brown uniforms on; air force people, no doubt. Occasionally someone in a gray uniform would appear and Carl guessed that he was a spaceship member but the person was too far away for Carl to get a good look at him.

After about 45 minutes the loading operation was complete since the trucks moved away and the door of the spaceship was closed. A few people went back and forth between the air force buildings and the spaceship during the next 15 minutes and then the lights on the loading platform went out. A little bit later the space craft lifted off the ground and slowly moved away. The only lights it had on were the few red and blue lights that it used when approaching the air force base.

Carl stood dumfounded for a while but decided that he was going to abandon his trip to Canyon City that night and follow any truck that left the base in an attempt to find out where it went. He figured that he might be able to determine what had been loaded on the spaceship if he could find out where the trucks had come from.

He went back to his car and switched on the radio. He didn't know how long he would have to wait before a truck left. Maybe hours. Finally, about 12:30am Carl saw a truck leaving the base and coming towards the highway. When it got to the highway, it turned towards Los Angeles. Carl started his engine and moved out, making a U turn on the highway with its wide shoulders at that point. He caught up to the truck in a couple of miles and started considering what approach to use. He couldn't just tail the truck for over a hundred miles; the truck driver would become suspicious. He decided that first of all he would make a mental note of the truck's license plate number and also its appearance. It had California license plate number W30498. It was a flat bed truck, black in color, about 40 feet long, and had FEULER mud guards over the back wheels.

Carl figured that the best thing, that he could do, would be to wait until the next lighted cross road came up and then pass the truck. He could get a pretty fair look at the cab and read the truck company's name on the door. He would then proceed ahead to the intersection of highways 395 and 15 and wait in the diner there for the truck to catch up. Accordingly, when Carl spotted an intersection up ahead he moved out to pass the truck. As he passed the cab, Carl read John Simmons, El Monte on the cab door. It was a dark green Mack tractor pulling the trailer.

Carl then continued on to the diner. It wasn't likely that the truck would turn off before reaching the diner as no major roads left the highway before the diner. Carl always liked the restaurant at the intersection of highways 395 and 15. On one wall someone had painted a mural of the Santa Fe Trail. The whole picture was actually a map of the southwest with little pictures of stage coaches and corrals and road houses along the way. The little pictures were out of scale, of course, but they gave a good idea of what things probably looked like around 1875. Carl took a seat by the window so he could watch for the approach of the truck. The truck driver didn't have to stop here of course, but it was two hours to the next major area and so it seemed likely that he would want to stop at this restaurant. Carl ordered a bowl of chili and a cup of coffee.

Presently the truck arrived, and sure enough the driver turned into the restaurant parking lot. When he entered the restaurant he sat at the counter. He was a civilian, probably about 40, and of average height. He wore an ordinary looking brown jacket with no company name on it. After two cups of coffee and a piece of pie he got up and walked over to the cash register to pay his bill.

Carl was trying to make up his mind on how to best tail the truck without attracting the notice of the driver. He couldn't just keep on driving up behind the truck, passing it, and then waiting up ahead for the truck to catch up. Sooner or later the truck driver would notice that. Carl decided at last that he would follow the truck but stay way back, just keeping the tail lights of the truck in view. If the truck turned off the highway, he could quickly catch up in order not to lose the truck.

Carl followed his plan for the next two and a half hours. He noted with interest that the truck did not go to El Monte, but rather went on down to Riverside. When it got to Riverside it turned into a mining company's big fenced-in yard. The sign on the fence read Anaconda Aluminum. Carl continued on home then to Newport Beach.

The next day Carl went to the library. He wanted to find out what products the Riverside Anaconda Aluminum plant produced. Was it just aluminum products? He didn't know exactly how to look it up but figured that he could begin by asking the librarian at the Business desk. Carl went directly to the desk with the Business sign above it. A dark haired man in his thirties with a blue shirt and red tie sat at the desk.

"Yes?" he asked when Carl approached.

"Can one find out what the products of a company are from books here in the library?"

"Sometimes," the man answered. "Which company did you have in mind?"

"The Anaconda Aluminum plant down at Riverside," answered Carl.

"I know of course that aluminum is their main product but I was wondering if they produce anything else down there. Can one find out that sort of thing around here?"

"You can look in the California Business Registry or the National Mining Registry," the librarian said, rising. Carl followed him to a shelf of thick manuals in one corner of the room. The man chose a book from a set of red volumes with the title California Business Registry on the binding. He paged through for a bit and presently declared, "Here we are. Anaconda Aluminum, Denver, Colorado: head office. Riverside, California facility: titanium refining, copper wire extruding, magnesium refining, and so forth. You can check this," he stated handing the book to Carl. Then moving to another shelf, he pulled a thick blue volume from a set and declared, "In the National Mining Registry we will certainly find something on Anaconda." He paged through the book and said, "Anaconda. Here it is. You can check this too. In the National Mining Registry, of course you'll find everything Anaconda does in the U.S. as well as abroad. You have to find the Riverside plant. Let's see." He was moving his finger down the page. "Here it is. Anaconda: Riverside, California. Their products are listed here," he indicated, handing the second volume to Carl. Carl thanked him, and the man returned to his desk.

Carl took the volumes to a table and checked them carefully. He discovered that the Riverside plant refined titanium, vanadium, manganese, and magnesium in addition to manufacturing copper wire. The next step was to check out a couple of books on metals. He could read them at his leisure and try to understand how Anaconda's products were used in industrial processes. He knew what some of the uses were but not all of them. Why would these things, or some of them, be shipped to another planet? Perhaps some of them were scarce on that other planet.

The next day was Sunday, and Carl went to church as usual. He always felt that he should go to church on Sundays.

Monday was a relatively clear day for Los Angeles. The Santa Ana wind had been active for the previous two days, and had blown quite a bit of the smog out to sea. Carl got an early start for Canyon City, and as he turned onto highway 15 after using highway 215 from San Bernardino the sky was clear and the air cool. A little over an hour later when Carl drove by Ellsworth Air Force Base, he carefully surveyed the area.

"I am going to find out what is going on out there," Carl decided.

The two day stretch at the Air Force station went as usual. Carl had to put assembly language code into the radar data acquisition section of the program to accommodate the new radar set that was being installed. He didn't particularly like programming but it wasn't too bad either. Occasionally it was interesting.

Tuesday night Carl was coming south on Highway 395 near the air force base and was straining hard to see if he could locate any red and blue lights in the sky. He didn't really expect to but couldn't help looking for them. Suddenly a man stumbled along the side of the road up ahead and started wandering on and off the road as he walked. He was just weaving around. He fell on the shoulder and Carl slowed down. He didn't know whether to stop or not but felt he ought to. The man was obviously in trouble and might need help. On the other hand he might be armed and dangerous. Carl toyed with the idea of just passing by and then later telephoning the police department.

As Carl came upon the man he noticed that he had on an air force uniform. Carl was relieved that he wasn't some dangerous crazy and decided to stop.

Carl rolled down his window and called, "Are you all right? Do you need help?"

The man looked up and stared for a moment and finally said, "Go on, I'm all right."

"How come your uniform is torn? Are you OK?"

The man looked carefully at Carl and his car and then walked up to the car. He was a young blond haired man in a torn officer's uniform. "Where are you headed?" he asked.

"I'm going down to L.A."

The man paused for a bit and asked, "Could you give me a lift that way?"

Carl opened the door. "Sure, get in."

"You look slightly injured," Carl said for openers. He pulled out and started down the road.

"I am," the man allowed, watching Carl intently. "My name is Ralph. Thanks for the lift."

"I'm Carl. Carl Johnson." Carl hesitated for a moment and then asked, "What do they do at that base? Or is it a big secret?"

"It's a secret all right. Wild, to say the least."

Carl wondered if he was going to explain his torn uniform. He didn't want to ask him outright. "It looks pretty small for airplanes," Carl said in an attempt to draw the man out into a discussion of the base's activities.

"I broke out of the brig tonight," Ralph said. "I tore my uniform climbing over the fence"

"You broke out of the brig!"

"Yeah, several of us were thrown in the brig a few weeks ago for talking about going to the newspapers."

"What's going on in there?" exclaimed Carl.

"It's weird, mister," Ralph looked carefully at Carl, apparently wondering if he should say any more. He looked forward down the road and asked if Carl had any cigarettes.

Carl took a pack from his pocket and reached them over.

"I'll tell you buddy, that's not a regular air force base over there. It's special duty and the rules don't apply." Ralph continued, "The other five guys and I were heard saying the wrong thing. That's all."

There was a long pause but Carl felt he shouldn't really say anything. Finally he said, "I work for General Engineering. We have a contract with the Defense Department at Canyon City and we have to go up there occasionally to service their radars."

The air force officer blew smoke out his open window. "I know about the Air Force flight test operation at Canyon City. In fact we have to monitor their air traffic so that their pilots don't see our visitors."

"Visitors?" Carl asked, thinking that he might be referring to the spaceship.

"Yeah, visitors."

"I saw something a little strange along here a few nights ago," Carl said, thinking he might be able to broach the subject of the spaceship now that the air force officer had mentioned visitors. "I was coming along here a few nights ago, Friday to be exact, and saw some colored lights approach that base. So I stopped and turned off my headlights and watched for about an hour." Carl glanced at Ralph to see how he was taking it. "It looked like a flying saucer to me."

There was silence for a minute and then Ralph said, "That's right. And nobody is supposed to know about it except a certain select few." He flipped his cigarette out the window.

Carl offered him the pack again and asked, "The air force knows about this? What's going on? Or, I suppose you are not supposed to say."

"Maybe I will tell it to a civilian now. That's what I was imprisoned for considering, anyway. The other guys and I were discussing going to a newspaper for quite a while. We were always careful to talk about it off base, confidentially, but I guess we were overheard someplace. Anyway, the air force decided it couldn't depend on us anymore and so we became a liability."

Ralph took a long drag and looked down the road for a while before continuing. "The Philadelphians, that's what they call themselves, are living on the Titan moon of Saturn. Their ancestors left earth on their way to Alpha Centauri in the year 2000 from this very base. It wasn't covered in the news or on television as well as the previous trips to the moon. The United States and several European countries were sending a colony to Alpha Centauri and decided to keep the endeavor well concealed."

"Why do you suppose they decided to keep it concealed?" asked Carl.

"I don't know," answered Ralph, "maybe they didn't want people to get angry over the expense of such an unnecessary trip. Most people would prefer to spend public money on their own communities rather than on an expedition to some distant planet."

"Why did they choose Alpha Centauri?" asked Carl. "They couldn't have known for sure that there were habitable planets in that sun system."

"They didn't know for sure," answered Ralph, "and they only surmised that there would be a habitable planet from astronomical observations. Besides, they didn't have many choices; I think that Alpha Centauri is the nearest sun. If there wasn't a suitable planet in the Alpha Centauri system, the astronauts could always come back."

"That would be a long trip for nothing," said Carl.

Ralph continued, "They had constructed two space ships here at this base that had nuclear powered engines.

The ships could travel for many decades without replacing their nuclear fuel rods. The engines could run constantly and thereby steadily accelerate the spaceships until they finally reached a velocity of one half or perhaps nine tenths the speed of light."

"So, at that speed, it would take at least four years to get to Alpha Centauri," remarked Carl.

Ralph went on, "Six hundred people from America, Canada, and several European countries boarded two space ships here in the year 2000. They took with them college text books, art works, Bibles, literature books, novels, and so forth."

"Anyway," continued Ralph, "they finally got to Alpha Centauri and found an acceptable planet to settle on."

"So they took a substantial piece of our culture with them," said Carl.

"Right," returned Ralph. "Six hundred people can form families and reproduce up to thirty or forty thousand people in 125 years. They use the name New Barstow for their colony in Alpha Centauri in honor of the California town, Barstow, which was near their point of departure from earth."

"They got into arguments over politics, economics, national origin, and language, and finally broke up their colony into separate states," continued Ralph. "They refer to New Barstow, in its entirety, as the Dynasty. Unfortunately, as is the custom with humans, they got into wars over land boundaries."

"Do you think they formed state boundaries out there?" asked Carl.

"Probably," answered Ralph. "I suppose if they didn't have wars as separate states they could have had a series of civil wars."

"So, what has all of this got to do with their base on the Titan moon of Saturn?" asked Carl.

"Well, as I was told, one of the states that constitute the New Barstow colony has the name New Philadelphia," answered Ralph. "New Philadelphia got into a war with the New Barstow government and New Philadelphia had their living space contaminated in a nuclear battle. The Philadelphians came back to our solar system, the earth's solar system, in an armada of very advanced space ships. They wanted to build a number of additional military space ships and then return to Alpha Centauri and acquire new living space on their planet in

Alpha Centauri. On their way to earth, they stopped on the Titan moon of Saturn and constructed a closed city there. This was about the year 2115. They set up their space ship factories on Titan."

"I suppose they would need a completely enclosed city on the Titan moon," said Carl. "It must be exceedingly cold and there is no oxygen to breathe."

"Yes. I think their enclosed city floats on a sea of liquid nitrogen," answered Ralph. "For a while they had all the building materials they needed for new space ships on their moon but they ran out of certain critical minerals and metals about a decade ago. They knew we had the minerals and metals and so they decided to use the manpower and industrial base of earth to supply them. They are way ahead of us technologically and we can't prevent them from taking what they want."

"How come we don't all know about it?" asked Carl. "Why don't they just come out in the open and demand the stuff. Why conceal it from the general public?"

"They feel, or rather our government feels, that it would be better for our society if the people didn't know that we were being controlled from outside. So a small number of key individuals in our government deal with the Philadelphians and keep everyone else in the dark."

Ralph had relaxed a bit and was apparently relieved at being able to finally let the story out into the open.

"How were the arrangements made?" began Carl. "I mean who decided to keep it a secret? Was it our government or those people?"

"As I heard it," answered Ralph, "they approached our government, some high ranking military officers at a base in Nebraska years ago, with their list of demands. And when those officers told our government the decision was made to keep it from the people. The government people figured that knowledge of such invaders would cause panic in the streets. So they tried to negotiate with the Philadelphians at the next scheduled meeting."

Ralph continued, "There wasn't anything our government could do. We had atomic weapons but the Philadelphians were so far ahead of us that they could cancel out our weapon systems with their superior battle cruisers. So the proposition that we would supply them with minerals if they would keep it quiet was put to them at Smith Air Force Base in Nebraska in 2115 and they accepted it"

"So they've been getting minerals from us ever since then. And the whole thing is done on the sly," said Carl.

"That's right," Ralph said. "I have also heard that a number of residents of California have noticed the spaceships when they drive by here, and their curiosity has led them to go up next to or even into the space ships. They were captured and taken along to the Titan moon. So, all together there are three groups of people involved: Barstonians, Philadelphians, and California prisoners."

Carl asked, "Well, do the Philadelphians on the Titan moon have weapon systems that can cancel out atomic explosions? What is their advantage over our weapons?"

"They have nuclear weapons, of course. In fact, I told you they drove themselves off their home planet in Alpha Centauri decades ago in a nuclear war. Their advantage lies in their delivery system and their ability to destroy our delivery system. They know where we are in our development but we don't know exactly where they are—except, that they are way ahead of us."

"What powers their spaceships?" asked Carl.

"They harnessed both fusion and fission nuclear power long ago and they use fission nuclear power for energy on their spaceships," answered Ralph. "They have all the energy they need back on their Saturn moon. They just ran low on magnesium and titanium and a few other metals. They take a lot of aluminum ingots; that's principally what they get from us."

"Do you suppose that our air force has considered sending a spy along on one of their spaceships to that moon to steal their technique for harnessing fusion power?" asked Carl.

"No doubt. But they know exactly how many air force people are at that base. Besides, they keep a contingent of troops there," replied Ralph.

"A contingent of troops! Do you mean that there are Philadelphian soldiers on that base here in California?" asked Carl.

"Right. Colonel Allerton and his platoon are on the base."

"What do they look like? I mean physically," asked Carl.

"They look like us, of course. They came from Europe and America a hundred and twenty five years ago. They seem to be a little taller and a little lighter in weight on average than us. Their uniforms are different.

The officers wear gray uniforms and the enlisted men wear blue uniforms.

Carl was silent for a while and then asked, "Do you suppose that there are some of them walking around among us in our towns?"

"I suppose so," answered Ralph. "They monitor everything we do, and consequently have to get close to the industrial processes in the factories if they are going to find out exactly how we do things."

Carl and the air force officer talked about the operations at Ellsworth Air Force Base and the spaceships for the next couple of hours. They stopped for ham and eggs and coffee at a restaurant along the way. Ralph didn't have any money so Carl paid for it. When they got to North Hollywood, Ralph said he would get out and proceed alone from there.

"What are you going to do now?" asked Carl. "You're AWOL. Are you going to the newspapers to tell your story, or what?"

"No, I'll probably go back to the base in a few days. They'll probably just put me in the brig for a few days, and then return me to duty."

They had stopped at the side of a street in Hollywood. "Thanks for the lift", said Ralph. "I wouldn't say anything or do anything if I were you. Those people will find some excuse for putting you in jail." With that he got out of the car, and with a wave of his hand he walked up Fifth Street.

Carl started the car and drove home to New Port Beach. When he got to his apartment, he got out his library books on metallurgy and started reading. He stayed up half the night reading. Carl found out that the three main ingredients of pig iron are iron ore, coke, and limestone. To make one ton of pig iron you need two tons of iron ore, one ton of coke (derived from coal), and one half ton of limestone. Pig iron is then made into various types of steel by adding small amounts of other substances. Varying amounts of manganese, vanadium, zirconium, tungsten, nickel, chromium, and molybdenum are added to pig iron to produce various types of steel. It didn't seem possible that the Philadelphians were making steel since that required a lot of coal, and coal is former living material. Carl couldn't remember anyone ever saying that there had been life on Saturn's moons.

One book stated that aluminum and magnesium might replace the age of steel by an age of light metals. However, it takes a lot of hydroelectric power to make aluminum from bauxite ore. Titanium is an excellent material for aircraft and spacecraft, but it is very expensive and titanium deposits aren't large.

Carl shut the book and tried to imagine what the closed city of the Philadelphians would look like. According to Ralph, the telemetry data from NASA's space probes to Saturn had been seized by the air force. The air force had subsequently released those portions that did not reveal the presence of the Philadelphians. Lieutenant General George Wilson, who was the air force officer in charge of the Philadelphian project, had seen to it that only those people who had to know about the Philadelphians received any information about them. Presumably, each successive president has been informed.

A closed, self contained city on the Titan moon of Saturn. Carl wondered if the Philadelphians were satisfied there or regarded it as only a temporary dwelling place. He had discussed that with Ralph, but nobody knew. Ralph assumed that the Philadelphians planned on returning to Alpha Centauri some time in the future. For the present they were using the planet earth as a client state, a supplier of raw materials.

Carl wondered if they would one day give up their intention of returning to Alpha Centauri, and instead descend to earth and take over a section of this country. Carl fell asleep dreaming of a city, enclosed in a glass dome, on a moon of the planet Saturn.

# Chapter 2

For the rest of the month of August, Carl worked on his second project. His second project was the design of a statistics program system that would allow a remote terminal user to access the statistics programs on the main computer and use the main computer's write-protected data base facility. He added a plotter and small printer at each terminal site. Also, he debugged some of the math routines.

By the second week of September, Carl was ready to leave for the Air Force site in the upper desert. Nancy Jones was going up too as she was ready to incorporate some program changes that she had been working on. So, they checked out a company car on Tuesday morning and set out. Nancy had a computer science degree from Stanford. She had short dark hair and gray eyes. Nancy liked bright colors. Today she wore a bright red blouse with her blue jeans. A few miles north of the plant, they came upon the large field of white boulders that Carl had always wondered about. There were thousands of boulders, about a foot or so in diameter, scattered through the field which extended for a long distance in both directions from the highway.

Carl asked, "Do you think that a river or glacier passed through this region on its way from the mountains to the ocean and deposited all these boulders?"

"It could have been an avalanche of some kind," answered Nancy.

Later on, they came to an abandoned winery.

Nancy said, "This winery has been used as a movie set several times. Its architecture is medieval, European and it can serve as a small baronial estate or a municipal building in a medieval town."

As they approached Ellsworth Air Force Base, Carl could not resist telling Nancy about his experiences of the previous month. He had refrained from speaking to anyone about it so far.

"Last month when I came along here, I had a strange experience," began Carl. "You have to promise not to tell this to anyone."

Nancy was looking at him, and with a slight grin, said, "Oh, what happened?"

"You have to promise not to talk about it. It might be dangerous."

Nancy looked at him more closely, and after a pause, said, "Dangerous. What do you mean?"

"I mean our government might not want you to tell anyone what you hear. That is, what I am going to tell you. Do you think you can be quiet about it?"

Obviously interested, Nancy answered, "All right, I won't say anything. What did you see?"

"Well—and you might think I am suffering from hallucinations, but I'm not—I saw a spaceship land here. Right here at this base. I was passing through here at night last month on my way to the Air Force base. Actually, at the time, I was parked on the side of the road up ahead a little, watching the stars." Carl paused a moment, and felt he would explain a little. "I sometimes stop and get out of the car at night and stare at the stars. They're so outstanding, here. Where I come from, it is usually overcast and we practically never see them this well."

"And so, you saw a flying saucer. Sure, you did. This job must be getting to you," returned Nancy with a smile, gently mocking him.

"Yeah, I know you won't accept it. But it's true anyway. I saw a spaceship land at that air force base over there, and they spent an hour, or so, loading it up with things—minerals and metals mostly, I think."

"You saw them loading a flying saucer with minerals," said Nancy incredulously. "You saw Air Force people, U.S. Air Force people, loading a flying saucer from outer space with our minerals. Come on, now, Carl. You're kidding me." Nancy obviously thought it was just a flimsy joke.

"I kid you not," returned Carl. "I was parked right about here, where we are now, and was looking at the stars when I saw some blue and reddish lights coming this way. I thought it was a helicopter and got the binoculars from the glove compartment. Then I could tell it wasn't a helicopter, but rather, a large spaceship. And, it landed at that base. They spent a long time—about an hour—loading it up, and then it took off. It rose very quietly, with a sort of humming sound. I followed a truck, which left the base, to try and find out what it was that they loaded onto the spacecraft. The truck went on down to Anaconda Aluminum near Riverside. I think they haul aluminum, magnesium, and perhaps titanium from Anaconda Aluminum to Ellsworth Air Force Base. I got a number of books at the library on the metal industry in an effort to understand what metals people from outer space would be interested in."

Carl was very excited about the whole thing. Nancy turned to watch him closely from time to time as he described what he had seen. It was an extraordinary tale, but he was obviously convinced of what he was saying. Carl also told her about Ralph, and what he had said. By this time Nancy was absolutely fascinated, and for the rest of the way to the Air Force base at Canyon City they discussed why the government would want to conceal such an operation. Carl was of the opinion that government people think that the government must always give the public the impression that their government is in charge of every situation. And, therefore, the government couldn't admit that there existed a situation beyond its control.

Late that afternoon, Nancy and Carl arrived at the Air Force base near Canyon City. They soon became involved in their respective computer program changes, and continued so for the next day. They didn't really have much of an opportunity to talk about the spaceship again until they were on their way back to Los Angeles.

After they had driven a ways, Nancy asked, "Do you think there will be another spaceship tonight?"

"I don't know," responded Carl. "It is about the same day of the month as it was when I came through here last time. Let's see, that was August 5th and today is September 9th. Of course, there is no reason to suppose that they make monthly trips. But, if they do, it's about the right time."

When they approached Ellsworth Air Force Base, they stopped on the same little hill overlooking the base on which Carl had stopped the previous month. It was about 10 pm.

They got out of the car and began scanning the sky for any sign of an aircraft or spacecraft.

"I brought my camera along," said Nancy. "I took it along in my luggage as I wanted to take pictures of the desert and flowers. When packing to return, I decided to put it in my handbag rather than in my overnight case. After what you said about that spacecraft, I wanted to have it ready," she said with a grin.

"Well, it's pretty unlikely that any spacecraft will come tonight," said Carl. "After all, what are the chances of our being here on just the right night for its arrival?"

It was a beautiful night and they enjoyed the pleasantness of the desert. After about an hour they decided to give up and leave. Nancy decided to take one last, careful scan of the sky before departing. She noticed a faint light moving, quite low in the sky, in the distance.

"What's that?" she said, pointing in the direction of the object. She thought that it was probably a private airplane.

"Where?" asked Carl, and looked in the direction she was pointing. It was far out and quite low, moving slowly. Just a light; one couldn't tell what color. Presently, they could distinguish several lights, and they realized that it was approaching.

"It's coming this way," breathed Nancy.

"You're right. Do you suppose that it is one of them? It would be an extraordinary coincidence, if it should occur on the second night that I am here," remarked Carl.

As the lights got closer, one could discern their color. Some were blue, while others were red. Carl had been watching through his binoculars, and said, "It's a spaceship. I can make it out now. It's another one!"

Nancy gasped with excitement. "Do you think I can get a picture with my camera?"

"We'll have to get closer," said Carl. "Your film won't be adequately exposed at night at this distance. Let's move up towards the base. We can move undetected in this sage brush and cactus until we get up near the base. There will no doubt be a fence up there that we can't get through, but you will be close enough to take a picture. Watch out for snakes as you move through this desert."

When they reached the base's perimeter fence, they had a pretty good view of the spaceship. It was very large, perhaps 500 feet across. It seemed larger than the one Carl had seen before. From the view they had of it, they couldn't decide what its basic shape was. It could be disk shaped, as they had always heard, or maybe ellipsoidal in shape. They figured that they had an edge-on view of the spacecraft.

Nancy started taking pictures when they got near enough. The lights on the loading dock had been switched on, and quite a few people were engaged in loading the spacecraft with boxes.

"Wouldn't it be tremendous if we could get close enough to get a clear picture of one of the crew members of that thing?" whispered Carl.

"It certainly would," exclaimed Nancy in a whisper.

They watched the proceedings with fascination for quite some time, waiting expectantly for someone in a uniform, different from a United States air force uniform, to appear. Finally, a person of somewhat more than average stature appeared in a gray colored uniform. He had on a helmet of some sort so they couldn't see his face but, they assumed that this was one of the crew members. The person went up to an air force officer, who was directing the operation, and apparently spoke to him. Presently, they went into one of the air force buildings.

Carl said softly, "Have you noticed how the air force people bring out a load of boxes on a fork-lift, load the boxes into the spaceship, and then go back into that building for about 5 minutes for another load? When they're in the building for that 5 minutes, nobody is out here.

He paused a second, swallowed, and continued, "We could actually get over this fence and get across to that spaceship—ducking behind those drums or barrels and that parked motor generator set—if we wanted to."

Nancy shook her head. "Let's not," she said. "We can see enough from here."

"If we could get over there," continued Carl, "we could take pictures of the inside of that thing. They would really be fantastic".

"No, let's not," repeated Nancy.

They watched the air force people bring out another load and transfer it to the spaceship.

When they left, Carl touched Nancy on the arm. "Come on, let's go," he said as he moved towards the fence. "Hurry up, let's get over the fence; we don't have much time. Be quiet."

Nancy was trying to stay back. "Stop, Carl. I'm not going in there," she was whispering.

When they got to the fence, Carl immediately started climbing. "Hurry up, we don't have much time, and don't drop the camera," he said.

By this time they were committed, and so, with trepidation and grumbling, Nancy followed. After climbing over the fence, they still had a distance of about 500 feet to go before reaching the spaceship. The loading dock was brightly lighted, but there were a lot of miscellaneous objects like boxes, drums, and a motor generator set to dodge behind and around in an attempt to conceal themselves.

Finally, they ducked breathlessly beside one of the spaceship's landing gears. They were trying to look in all directions at the same time, as they moved, in order to avoid stepping into anybody's field of vision. Carl thought that the safest thing to do would be to get up inside the spaceship where they could conceal themselves in the passageways or behind things, rather than just standing where they were on the loading dock.

"Come on, let's go inside before that loading crew returns. We can hide in one of those passageways," Carl said, gesturing towards a labyrinth of passages leading away from the spaceship's freight storage bay.

Nancy groaned, but they were committed now and so they moved as rapidly as they could to a ladder extending from the ground up into the spaceship. When they reached the top of the ladder, they slipped as quickly as they could behind a loading crane of some sort. They scanned the place rapidly, looking for any crew member or anything that looked like a window from which they could be seen.

"Let's try and find the engine room and see what makes this thing go" whispered Carl.

"How are we going to find that. We can't read their signs," answered Nancy with a mild note of ridicule in her voice.

"You're right. Let's just look around and take some pictures. Maybe we will just come upon the engine room after a while" After a pause, he continued, "You know, if we could find a book or manual in one of these rooms with pictures and equations in it, we could take photographs of it with your camera—provided that your camera can focus on pages of print. And then, tomorrow, we could match recognizable pictures and equations on the one hand with the words we find on those pages on the other hand, and thereby start a dictionary of their language," Carl said.

"Why? Let's just get out of here," replied Nancy with annoyance.

"It would be an effective way to translate a language from outer space. It would be similar to the way some Frenchman deciphered hieroglyphics by comparing two descriptions of the same events or ideas printed next to each other on the Rosetta Stone, one in a known language and the other in an unknown language," replied Carl.

They set out down one of the corridors, being very circumspect in their movements less they be seen by somebody. There didn't seem to be anyone around.

"I wonder if they are watching us on little television like, monitors," said Nancy.

"They might have sensors all over the place that record anybody moving about, and a central monitoring station from which they can view everything," added Carl.

They slipped into the first room that they came to. It didn't have a door. The room had a couple of alcoves or recesses in the walls that served as work tables. A few instruments were on the tables. A drawer, built into the wall, near one of the tables was partly open. Carl peered in and saw only a collection of instruments.

"Let's open some of these drawers and see if we can find anything recognizable," he whispered to Nancy.

They opened a number of drawers, but all they found were test tubes and apparatus for chemical or biological procedures. No literature of any sort. Near one of the tables was a CRT screen with some writing displayed on it.

"What if they don't have manuals, but keep all their information in a computer data base and just bring it up on the screen when they need it," said Nancy; "That would save a lot of space and weight on a spaceship like this."

"What we could do, if we are careful," said Carl, "is to try and call up some things on the screen. Maybe, we can find what we want that way."

"Do you want me to try typing in something on this?" asked Nancy, examining the screen with its set of keys on the wall.

"Yes, but don't press any of those red buttons," said Carl. "They might be some kind of alert, or rather, request for help keys, and the last thing we want now is for an assistant to come to our aid."

Nancy smiled and gave a little grunt of agreement, and began examining the keyboard configuration without touching anything.

"I feel like a beginning programmer, facing a terminal for the first time," she said with a smile. "I suppose if I just try a few things it won't hurt anything and it probably won't sound an alarm. After all, they aren't expecting invaders on this spaceship," she said.

So she started experimenting with the keyboard. For a while nothing happened. Finally she hit a combination of keys that caused a different pattern to appear on the screen.

"Do that again," said Carl;

Nancy repeated the combination, and the pattern changed again.

"Should I keep it up until something interesting or understandable appears?" she asked.

"Yes, go ahead," answered Carl.

After a few minutes she turned up something that looked like a map. She paused and said, "Do you suppose that we have a layout of the spaceship?"

"Maybe. Get the next one up. Maybe it will give the outline of the spaceship. We can't tell which portion of the ship is on this map," answered Carl.

She brought up some more pictures, using the keys, until finally one appeared that contained the outline of the ship. They went back and forth between the pictures, until they located themselves on the set of maps.

"That big thing there in the middle must be the engine," said Carl, pointing to a large shape situated in the middle of the ship's outline on one of the maps. "It's probably a very heavily shielded reactor and must be placed at the center of gravity of the spaceship in order to maintain stability," he continued. "If we could get there and take a few photographs, we would have something valuable. Maybe they will have a manual down there too, who knows," he said. "Then we will have to get off this thing."

"OK. If we are here," Nancy said pointing at the screen, "we can follow this passage to the engine, or whatever it is."

They proceeded down the passageway, outside the room they had been in, according to a mental picture they had formed from the map on the CRT screen.

"This place gives me the creeps. Nobody is around. They must have sensors or little TV cameras someplace," said Nancy.

Just then she noticed what appeared to be a viewing camera mounted in the ceiling at the intersection of their passageway with another passageway up ahead. She stopped short and pointed at it. They watched it turning in a regular, repetitive motion. "We can duck under it when it's pointing to the left, and then hurry to the right, and then down the passageway to a place of concealment."

When the camera passed where they were crouched in a doorway and started on its leftward motion, they hurried to the passageway intersection, took a quick glance each way, and darted to the right. They made it to a recessed doorway before the camera made a sweep in their direction.

Just then they heard sounds coming down the passageway and they stepped back into the room. Two crew members passed by, talking to each other. They wore light gray uniforms, but they didn't wear helmets or hats of any kind. Nancy and Carl got only a fleeting glimpse. They had dark brown hair, light colored skin, and ordinary looking European facial features.

"They resemble a lot of people on earth," whispered Nancy.

When the two crew members had passed, Nancy and Carl continued on their way. The surprising thing was how empty the ship was. There was a lot of room, but not many people.

"I suppose an ocean going freighter is big and fairly empty like this, too," said Carl. "You need a lot of room to store things but only a few people to run the ship."

They finally found the room with the big object that they had seen on the CRT screen. The object, or engine if that is what it was, was cylindrical in shape and gave off a low pitched humming sound. On one wall was a control panel with lots of gauges and controls.

"This must be the engine room, and those are the engineers' controls on the panel over there," said Carl. "You need a lot of room but only a few people to run the thing."

As they approached, they noticed a number of manuals or books in a book case that had been built into the wall. Carl pulled one out and riffled through it.

"Do you think you could take photographs of these pages with your camera?" Carl asked Nancy.

"It has an adjustable lens, and I have taken pictures of bugs on flowers with it," Nancy said. "We could try it. Perhaps the negatives could be blown up later so that we could read the pictures."

"OK. Take a picture of these three pages. I recognize some of the equations and diagrams. So, maybe we can use the equations along with the other words on the pages to start building our dictionary," said Carl.

"I only have fourteen frames left on this film," said Nancy. "So this will use three of them."

When she finished, she said, "I'll get one of the engine, and then let's get out of here."

They left the room, planning to retrace their steps.

"I wouldn't mind having a picture of the control room or pilot's cabin before we leave here," said Carl.

"Maybe we can find another CRT terminal and look up its location," Nancy said.

They went down the passageway, peering into every room in search of another terminal. About half way back to their place of entry into the ship, they found a room with a lot of electronic subassemblies lying on benches, and a terminal on one wall.

"Let's try this terminal," said Carl, entering the room.

It was apparently a repair shop or workshop for electronic assemblies from every part of the spaceship. Lots of devices of all shapes and sizes were there, and although most of it was unrecognizable there were typical looking dials, switches, and gauges on the front panels of some of the devices.

Nancy was at the terminal working her magic on the keyboard. She managed to turn up the maps on the screen again, and they started scanning the maps for a possible control center or pilot's cabin when they heard voices in the passageway.

"Quick, let's get behind these cabinets," said Carl.

Two crew members pushed a cart into the room with a device of some kind on it. They hoisted the device onto a table, talking all along in their smooth, mellow sounding language. After strapping the device down to the table, they departed. Outside in the passageway, one of them pushed a key that he was carrying into a hole in the wall, and to Nancy and Carl's horror a door came down from the ceiling to the floor, barring their exit from the room.

They rushed to the closed door.

"There must be a corresponding hole in the wall on this side into which one can insert a key," said Nancy. "But we don't have a key!"

Her eyes were wide with terror as she looked at Carl. He swallowed and said nothing. They began frantically looking around for a key or anything that might serve as a key.

After several minutes of futile searching, Nancy began to cry and said, "What will we do now?"

"I don't know," answered Carl. "If we pound on the door somebody will probably come to let us out, but then they might put us in a prison."

"We can't stay here. We don't know where they are going. We will be going into outer space," said Nancy with a shaky voice. "What shall we do?"

Carl comforted her as best he could, but he wasn't feeling any better himself. He realized that he would have to calm himself down and think clearly. Frenzied activity wouldn't do them any good.

Finally, he said, "We are better off going along as stowaways to their planet and returning with them next month than making ourselves known now and, as a result, being thrown into prison. We can keep out of sight in this huge, empty ship and return to earth next month. Even if a round trip takes several months, we are better off spending those several months as stowaways than being caught now. It could be that the reason why a spaceship arrives on earth every month is that there are several spaceships on this route."

After a few moments of reflection, Nancy agreed that that was all they could really do.

"What will we eat on this spaceship for a month?" she asked. "We can hide, but we have to eat something. What if their food is poisonous to us? I mean, if we eat the excess food they throw away in their kitchen, we might get sick."

"We will have to take the chance. We don't have much choice," answered Carl.

Presently, they could feel the room vibrating slightly, and it felt as though they were going up slowly in an elevator.

"I guess we are taking off," said Carl.

Nancy was silent; she just looked at Carl.

# Chapter 3

Nancy and Carl's first order of business was to find a place on the spaceship where they could live without being detected. They had managed to get out of the electronic assembly repair room, in which they had been locked, by using some tools in the room to fabricate a key to the locked door. Before leaving the room, Nancy had brought up the ship's anatomy on the CRT screen and they had drawn a map of the ship on a piece of paper. An important consideration in selecting a living site was to be near the spaceship's fresh water and plumbing systems and not too far from the ship's galley. Nancy and Carl discovered that on a large spaceship there were many utility systems, such as fresh water, plumbing, electrical, and ventilation.

On their way down to the garbage bay to intercept their evening meal on its way from the galley to the garbage cans, Carl got to talking about his favorite new project: making a dictionary of the Philadelphian language.

"We are going to have to make a calendar and also figure out their language," Carl said. "Otherwise, we won't know what's going on and we will lose track of time."

"What difference does it make what the date is?" asked Nancy.

"I want to maintain my orientation in earth's affairs, and I can't do that very well without a calendar," answered Carl.

"Do you really think, then, that we are going to return to earth?"

"Of course," replied Carl with more confidence in his voice than he actually felt. "They go back and forth to get minerals, and we are going to be on a return ship some day. But we will be safer and more successful if we know their language, because then we will know what they are saying and thinking."

"Are you going to make your dictionary just from those technical manuals we found in the engine room? Because, if you are, we won't be able to understand much of their casual, ordinary speech," said Nancy.

"I'll use more than just those manuals. I shall write down, in some fashion, the sounds they say over the loud speaker system, and then I'll watch what they do. In that way, I can attach or assign a meaning to the action or sounds. I ought to be able to match some of their sounds with the words we find on the CRT screen," Carl said.

"Perhaps you can match some of their actions with the words on the screen," said Nancy.

"Yes, I'll watch what they do, what they say, and what is written on the CRT screen. Sometimes I ought to be able to make some direct comparisons, like for example when a sentence flashes up on the screen and then we see some of them go and do something or say something," said Carl. "We might be with these people for a year or two and we will be better off if we can tell what they are saying."

"Here's the garbage dump," said Nancy. "I wonder what's for supper tonight."

"We're like dogs," said Carl. "That brown and white stuff last night wasn't too bad."

"Do you mean the plastic beef," asked Nancy with a grin.

They were crouching behind one of the stanchions when the galley attendant with his push cart came into view.

"Here is Raymond," said Carl. They had started assigning names to the members of the crew. "He is lackadaisical as usual. These people are typical humans."

Raymond pushed his cart, containing galley refuse, up to the door opposite Nancy and Carl. He was wearing a casual gray jumper shirt and blue pants with white soft-sole shoes. His thin arms showed since he had rolled up his shirt sleeves, and his dark hair was messed as usual. The crew members in the control room all had regulation hair cuts and always wore neat uniforms with their insignia on the collar and their rank on the upper sleeve. Raymond's smooth face, with its small nose and mouth, looked bored and indifferent to the day's events. He had been slouching over his cart as he advanced along the passageway.

Carl and Nancy kept silent behind their stanchion in the passageway as Raymond opened the door to the garbage bay and entered. They knew that he would dump the garbage onto a long conveyer belt that would carry it to a chemical decomposition machine. The machine would convert the garbage into a white powder, and then eject it in closed containers. The cooks would return after several hours to pick up the containers; they used the white powder to make new plastic-beef, spinach, jell-o, or whatever.

As soon as Raymond had disappeared from sight down the passageway, Nancy and Carl darted through the door into the garbage bay, bowls in hand, to intercept the garbage on the conveyer belt before it reached the chemical decomposition machine.

"Ah, carrot-jell-o and cardboard-mutton for tonight," said Carl.

"Yes, and for dessert, strawberry shortcake," exclaimed Nancy as she scooped up some red jam like stuff and a piece of hard tack bread.

They made their way back through the labyrinth of passageways to their place of dwelling in the cargo bay. It was clean and quiet in their corner of the cargo bay, and there were no sensors or scanners nearby. A watchman came through once a day, but he followed a schedule and Nancy and Carl could prepare for it.

They had arranged some boxes containing spices and fine textiles—the Philadelphians valued those as well as minerals—into a kind of room for themselves. They had to climb several levels of boxes to get to their dwelling place.

Nancy had made some couches and chairs and two beds by piling bolts of soft velvet material on the floor. For a shower they used a valve in one of the water mains on the third level where nobody ever seemed to pass. They figured that turning on a valve in a water main for a few minutes would go undetected in the control room. They fashioned a bathroom out of what had been intended as a small utility room; the utility room had been built with fresh water pipes leading to it, and drainage pipes leading from it to the plumbing system. It was only about 200 feet from their dwelling place.

Carl pulled the curtains closed over the entrance to their living quarters and switched on the light that he had rigged to the electric power lines.

"I wish we had some form of home entertainment here like a television set or a sound system for playing music," he said.

"We ought to try and develop a taste for their music," said Nancy. "We could just put one of their intercom units in here and use headphones."

"When I get my dictionary and grammar book written," said Carl with a sense of confidence, "we will be able to understand their sentences. Maybe they have interesting stories on that intercom system as well as music, after hours."

"What could their stories be about?" asked Nancy as she came over to sit by Carl.

"Oh, I don't know. Maybe they have various Sagas to relate. Maybe love stories," said Carl.

"Wow," said Nancy playfully. "Love stories," she said with a smile as she snuggled up.

"Yes, love stories; why not?" responded Carl, as he put his arm around her.

She smiled and laughed a little. They talked for a while about going out on dates when they eventually return to earth.

Carl was lying awake on his cot, staring at the boxes, and thinking about his dictionary when he heard Nancy stir on her cot.

"I am going to start my dictionary and grammar book by making an alphabet of their letters and by listing a few of their words, whose meanings are easy to guess. I can deduce the meanings of quite a few words from the formulas in which they use the words. For example, when they give the voltage and current or power rating for a device, I can figure out which words stand for ampere and volt just from their location in the formula," he said.

"Dictionary, again," said Nancy as she sat up on her cot.

Carl reached for his watch and wound it. He made a mark on his calendar and said, "I wonder what's for breakfast."

"Probably hot brown bread and orange eggs, as usual," murmured Nancy. She sat on her cot with her elbows on her knees and her chin cupped in her hands, regarding him. "How come we never went out on dates, down on earth?"

"Well, when we get back we will," said Carl, smiling at her.

While sitting on the edge of his cot and contemplating the day ahead, Carl continued, "I think that I'm going to scrounge around in that repair room we found the other day for a camera and a voice recorder. Probably, neither one will work; in fact, that's why they would be there. But maybe I can get them to work. Your camera will be out of film soon. We need one of their cameras, which I think are digital cameras."

"What are you going to use the voice recorder for? Are you going to sneak up behind the guards, and try to record their conversation?" asked Nancy, laughing.

"I don't know yet how I'll use the sound stuff, but maybe it will come in handy. These people are way ahead of us, and I am going to snoop around with camera and microphone in hand and take down all I can. I am a natural spy, I guess."

"Well we don't have much time, maybe just a few more days, if we're going to one of the moons of Saturn," Nancy said.

"No, but we can move about on Titan and gather information and then stowaway on a return trip," said Carl.

"Do you think that we can move about without attracting attention?" asked Nancy.

"We look like them, but we have to learn to talk and act like them."

"You can dye your dark hair a shade of blond, and we can wear that kind of eye glasses that some of them wear. If we don't go right up and speak to them, they probably won't notice our difference. We're a little shorter, but if we don't stand next to them they probably won't notice."

"Do you suppose that we can learn their language in a short time," asked Nancy.

"Well, we can try," replied Carl. "In the mean time, I would like to get copies of their engine specifications and schematics. This spaceship took off without blasting away. Somehow it works directly against gravity. Its acceleration is not due to the reactive force from blasting off mass, as in a chemical rocket engine."

Nancy and Carl spent the next two days in the repair shop. They found a large copy machine, from which they were able to remove the camera. The camera would enable then to take pictures of schematics and printed pages in engineering manuals. Getting into the supply store room to obtain film required some ingenuity as that place was carefully supervised. They timed their movements to coincide with the times when the store room attendant went to the front desk to confer with people who came in to requisition supplies.

In the engine room they timed their movements to accommodate the strict regimen that the engineers followed. They noticed that the engineer on duty would operate a number of controls on the main console and then go over to the various gauges and printouts in the room to monitor the engine's performance. When he was away from the console, Carl and Nancy would remove a book or set of schematics from a shelf or drawer and then retreat to their hideout in a sort of closet to film the papers. On one of the engineer's absences from the main console, Carl would replace the documents and borrow another set. They took as many pictures of the engine itself as they dared, with the engineer in the room. Nancy and Carl carried radiation detectors with them when they went near the engine, but they found that the radiation level was negligible.

Of course they couldn't develop the film on the spaceship, but they figured they could do so later when they arrived on the planet, Titan. In the meantime they would film as much as they could.

# Chapter 4

Nancy awoke Carl early one morning with a shake. "We must be arriving at Titan," she said. "The ship's been creaking under stress and I've sensed deceleration off and on for the last hour."

Carl sat up and started dressing. "Let's hurry and take a look out the window in the upper storage bay," he said.

They scrambled up to the window they had found on the second night out. They had always enjoyed watching the stars from it. The view of Titan was clear and fine. The huge Saturn moon was pale orange in color, and its thick cloud cover obscure its surface features. Nancy and Carl noticed a number of fast moving escort ships dashing about. They began their descent through the cloud cover, and soon they could discern certain land features.

"That must be where we are headed," said Nancy, pointing in the direction of several straight roads or paths with small buildings or structures near them.

As they approached the site, the shape of the buildings became more apparent. The entire city or post was enclosed within a large transparent dome with numerous vertical pillars supporting it. There were no bright or prominent colors. The buildings were light brown in color, evidently having been constructed from the materials found in the surface crust of Titan. They were approaching a structure that looked like an entrance gate.

"That must be where we are going to land," said Nancy, pointing to the structure directly ahead. "The lights on it are starting to flash. Maybe they're landing pattern lights."

"Come on, let's get our things together," said Carl. "We'll try to slip out when the opportunity presents itself."

They returned to their living site and started packing their films and papers. The bolts of cloth were returned to the boxes from whence they came. They tidied up the whole area. It wouldn't do for the Philadelphians to discover that there had been stowaways on board.

It was not difficult for Nancy and Carl to get into the Philadelphian base unseen. They simply opened a pallet of textiles and made a little compartment for themselves inside the case. Then they closed up the plastic cover and secured it with some tape. They figured that the pallet would be stored in a warehouse and that they could get out at their leisure. As it turned out they were out of their packing crate in an hour. They found themselves in a large warehouse, possibly a thousand feet on a side.

"Come on," said Carl, "I want to get a look at this place." He took Nancy by the hand and tugged her along.

"All right, all right, take it easy," Nancy said. "We've got plenty of time, probably too much time."

They didn't see anyone in the warehouse, and got up to a door without any trouble. Carl pushed the door open slowly, and peered out through the crack.

"Only a few people are moving about in this part of town," said Carl. "I suppose we might as well call it a town, for lack of a better expression," he added.

"What does it look like out there?" asked Nancy with excitement.

"There are a number of ordinary buildings, probably not dwellings. There are windows, but I don't see anyone in them," answered Carl. "There is a car, or vehicle of some sort, coming. Right after it passes, let's step out onto the street and go to the left. There are only a few people walking out there, and they won't be coming towards us."

They were walking on the side of a driveway or street. The buildings were low and were all constructed from brown bricks. The bricks were no doubt made from the clay of the moon.

"We'll have to get some clothes like these people wear pretty soon so we won't be conspicuous," said Nancy.

"Yes. Isn't the sky fantastic!" said Carl. "Look at Saturn up there," nodding at the enormous ball in the sky above their heads.

"Gives me the creeps," said Nancy. "Everything is so foreign."

"You can just make out the glitter of the transparent dome above our heads," said Carl. "Don't you feel lighter as you walk on this moon? The gravity here is substantially less than on earth."

"Yes. We had better plan where we are going, and also be circumspect in our movements, as we are coming to an intersection up ahead," Nancy said, "and we might run smack into somebody."

"Watch for a clothing store," Carl said. "We have to get some clothing like theirs so we won't be conspicuous. Of course we don't have any money, but maybe they issue clothing here in the same way that it is issued in an army."

When they got to the intersection, they stepped out smoothly and unhesitatingly so as not to attract attention. There were a lot of people milling about and going in and out of various buildings. As Nancy and Carl passed the doorways, they peered in. It was hard to tell what the buildings were used for. The people just entered them and disappeared down hallways. They finally came to a group of shops or stores. The people were standing around inside some of them, looking at various items on shelves and tables.

Nancy grabbed Carl's arm. "Look over there," she said, nodding to the right. "Those people are taking things from a table and holding them up to themselves before mirrors, just as we do with a shirt or dress when we want to see how we look in it."

Carl looked in the direction in which she was indicating. They moved over to the door of the shop and glanced in. They pretended to be talking to each other, and Nancy stood facing the door so that she could look in.

"They aren't using money or anything like it," she said after a few minutes. "They seem to have some sort of card that they hand to a clerk when they want something, and the clerk just inserts the card into a machine and then gives it back. Here comes somebody with her purchase, or whatever you want to call it."

They moved away slightly when the person reached the door. She walked out with a red coat or sweater under her arm. The new garment hadn't been wrapped or put in a bag.

"The trouble is that we don't have a card either," said Carl. "I wonder what they do with their discarded clothing. We've been eating their garbage for food; maybe we can wear their discards for clothing."

"Well, let's find where they live and look for their trash cans," said Nancy.

They set off, moving in the same direction that the majority of the people were walking. Occasionally, a vehicle would pass by. It seemed to be a kind of electric car. The people were friendly toward one another and chatted freely.

"They really look a lot like us, don't they?" said Carl; "They act about the same way, too. I mean the way they gesture and talk with each other."

"Yes, I agree," said Nancy. After a moment, she continued, "Those larger buildings on the right up ahead must be office buildings or factories."

As they got nearer to one of the buildings, they could see what appeared to be small spaceships behind it.

"Maybe it's a spaceship factory," said Carl. "Look at all the spaceships behind that building." After a pause, he continued, "They're kind of small; they can't go a very long distance. I wonder if they are carried aboard a big spaceship and then launched for short missions, or something."

"I don't know," murmured Nancy, looking at the ships.

The next building had a lot of windows and was a little smaller. "I wonder what they make in there," said Carl.

"Look at that complex of small structures, or boxes, up ahead," said Nancy. "It looks like a living habitat. Each box could be a single home. They're all sort of stuck together at different angles and piled several stories high."

"It must be their living quarters," said Carl. "Let's go that way, and look for discarded clothing."

As they approached the site, they noticed children playing. They used sticks and a ball in a game resembling polo. As Nancy and Carl walked by the complex, a truck came out of one of the driveways, but they couldn't tell what was in it. The people on the street were apparently going through their everyday routines. The children played and yelled and could be heard crying here and there. Some adults could be seen talking to their neighbors on the little porches or verandas attached to the boxes. When Nancy and Carl reached the next corner, they noticed some large containers down the side street.

"Maybe those are the trash cans," said Carl.

"Ah, our clothing bazaar and dining facility," said Nancy, ruefully.

"Yes, I am afraid so," returned Carl. "Let's wait until dark to do our shopping."

"Where are we going to live in this town?" asked Nancy.

"Good question," replied Carl. "If I could get some kind of job around here, I could acquire one of those cards they use for obtaining food and clothing and maybe even houses."

"How can you get a job around this place?" asked Nancy. "You look like them, but you certainly don't speak like them."

"Yes, but I have been studying their language and compiling my dictionary, and I understand quite a bit of what they say," returned Carl. "And, with my sound recorder I can learn to imitate their voice inflections."

"But, what are we going to do in the meantime"

"I guess we'll just have to live in the back of one of those big warehouse buildings, and feed on garbage," answered Carl.

With that, they turned around and retraced their steps, dejectedly, to the large warehouses. They selected one that was nearly full, and consequently wouldn't be entered too many more tines by the Philadelphians. Nancy and Carl managed to build tolerable living quarters on the third floor of the building. They found a cluster of pallets that had been placed tightly together in a rectangular array in the middle of the floor. So, they climbed to the top of the rectangular cluster, and removed the contents of the middle four pallets, thus hollowing out a space for themselves. They just stacked the materials, that they had removed, in a different place on the floor. The Philadelphians had stored mostly plastic like building materials and various kinds of textiles on the third floor of the building. Nancy and Carl draped the walls of their hollowed out space with attractive fabrics that they found in some of the boxes. They made two beds by piling bolts of cloth on the floor, and fashioned a table and chairs from the plastic building materials.

After Nancy and Carl had been on Titan a few days, they noticed that the Philadelphians had set the day at twenty five hours in duration. The Philadelphians established the day through the use of clocks and artificial lighting; they ignored the natural periods of light and darkness that were observable through the transparent roof of the dome in which they lived. The natural periods outside the dome were too short. Carl figured that the Philadelphians had chosen a twenty five hour day because the natural period of day and night on their home planet was twenty five hours. This suggested that their home planet was about the same size as earth and about the same distance from its sun as earth is from its sun. Nancy and Carl noticed, furthermore, that the Philadelphians tended to sleep eight hours of their twenty five hour day, work eight hours, and spend the rest of the day in recreation or in educational classes.

Nancy and Carl learned the Philadelphian language quite easily. They went out and moved about quietly and unobtrusively, taking note of the words people used to describe things, and being particularly careful to mark their pronunciation. Carl's dictionary was growing rapidly.

They culled enough old clothing from trash cans to enable themselves to dress like the other people. Nancy died her hair brown and Carl fabricated a set of brown framed glasses for himself.

They yearned for the new things that they saw in the store windows, and often discussed the possibility of Carl finding employment so that he might be issued a purchasing card. One morning Carl said, "I think I am going to apply for an electrician or electronics technician job. I have studied all those wiring diagrams and schematics that we found in the spaceship, and I think that I could pass any written entrance examination or verbal interview."

"You ought to be able to do that kind of work for them; you're very adept at it," replied Nancy. "Where are you going to apply?"

"I noticed a job advertisement for a municipal electrician on a bulletin board in one of the buildings the other day," said Carl. "A list of available jobs is posted every twelve days on the bulletin board, and each advertisement states the building and room number where you apply," he continued. "I could give 150 Tilcor as an address on an application form; that's the number on the door of that vacant apartment we noticed the other day at that housing development called Tilcor," Carl said. "It's a little risky, but I suppose I'll have to give an address on an application form. And, besides, perhaps we can get that apartment if I get the job," he said.

"What will we use for names?" asked Nancy.

"I don't know. What do you think?" asked Carl.

"How about Reh and Dora Sans?" answered Nancy. "Those seem to be fairly common names here, I've noticed, and I like the way they sound," she said with a smile.

"Reh and Dora Sans sounds great to me," Carl said, looking at Nancy. He put his arm around her and gave her a hug. He was becoming very fond of her.

On the appointed day, everything went smoothly. Carl had to fill out an application form and pass a written test. He also had to demonstrate his competence by repairing a circuit in the presence of a proctor, who had previously rendered the circuit inoperable by damaging a component. Following that, Carl had a short interview with a placement official. The official assigned Carl the position of electrician at Factory 8, the factory that produced the small spaceships. Since Factory 8 was quite a distance from the Tilcor housing complex, Nancy and Carl were assigned dwelling 165 at the Montan housing complex.

"Well, we got a legitimate house and shopping card," Carl announced as he returned home.

He was rather proud of himself. He had passed all the tests and nobody suspected anything. Nancy was extremely pleased and gave him a big kiss.

"Let's go look at the house right after we eat," she said. "When can we move in and use our card?" she asked, excitedly.

"Right away. Let's move tomorrow but go look at it today," answered Carl. "I've got to report to work in three days the placement guy said. I don't think they suspect anything."

"They're probably so sure of their security system that they don't expect any unauthorized people to be around," Nancy suggested.

"Yes, you're probably right."

They had a nondescript casserole for supper and a vegetable and fruit salad. The Philadelphians had imported vegetable and fruit seeds from earth and constructed an artificially lighted building in which to grow them. Nancy had become quite a good cook and the casserole wasn't bad even if the ingredients were foreign.

After supper they walked over to 165 Montan. The door was unlocked so they walked into the vacant apartment. It consisted of a living room, kitchen, bathroom, and bedroom. Nancy and Carl had been surprised from the start how similar Philadelphian furniture was to earth furniture. They realized, of course, that this was to be expected since the Philadelphians had originally come from earth. The Philadelphians even had pictures but they were pictures evidently of their original homeland. Nancy and Carl noticed that the pictures didn't depict anything on Titan. Some of the scenes showed two moons.

"Boy, we can move in here tomorrow. Fantastic!" exclaimed Nancy.

"Certainly is an improvement over our hideaway in the warehouse," responded Carl.

"Even the view isn't bad," continued Nancy, looking out the window, "and look at all the furniture and rooms. A real house," she said with a wide and happy grin.

They returned to their warehouse hide out, walking hand in hand down one of the town streets.

Carl started his new job on the scheduled day. He didn't have to work closely with anybody and therefore his accent wasn't very noticeable. Only at the beginning of the shift and at the end of the shift did he have to mingle with the others, and at those times he tried to keep a distance whenever possible. His brown framed glasses were quite good and his hair color was fine. But, he was afraid his accent would give him away. He paid close attention to the conversation of the others in order to pick up the voice inflections and nuances of word meaning.

Nancy and Carl would frequently discuss the idioms and pronunciations at home. Carl tried hard to steer clear of the government police when they would pass through the area. They had a way of staring at a person, which was very disconcerting, and Carl always thought they suspected something.

Carl's job as municipal electrician took him into the factory that made the small spaceships, mainly, but occasionally he would get an assignment in one of the other factories or municipal buildings.

Carl always carried his miniature camera with him and took pictures of any schematics or blueprints that he thought would be useful to earth people—if he ever got back. He was particularly interested in the power plants or engines used in the spaceships. He wanted to find out how these people had managed to use gravity as a mode of transportation rather than the standard chemical engines of people on earth or even the reactor engines used by people on earth.

One night while on an assignment in the spaceship factory to fix an electric power line to a certain bank of machinery, Carl was as usual spending time over by the manuals describing the spaceship engines. He was reading the material and photographing the pages when he heard a sound back in one of the bays, like a tool falling to the floor. Carl quickly slipped back to the electric switch box he was supposed to be working on.

A little while later one of the government police officials passed by and said, "Good evening, Sir. I am just making my rounds. Have you seen anything out of the ordinary?"

Carl answered, "No. I have noticed nothing unusual."

Carl wasn't sure if the policeman had seen him over by the manuals or not. Carl figured that if he had been seen away from the electric switch board, that a report would be filed at the police station even if nothing was immediately done. Carl resolved to be much more careful in the future.

He told Nancy about the encounter that night.

"Well where was he when you heard the thing drop?" asked Nancy. "Was it far behind you in another room or nearby?"

"The tool, or whatever it was, hit the floor probably about 200 yards or so behind me," said Carl. "It was in the same room but it's a huge room with lots of machinery in it. He might not have seen me."

"But he could have," said Nancy.

"Yes, he could have. But how would he know that I was supposed to be by the electric switch boxes and not by that table with the manuals on it?"

"Could he check some way what your assignment is?" asked Nancy.

"Oh, I suppose, but a lot of electricians are nosy and root around where they have no business."

After a pause Nancy said, "Well be careful in the future," and squeezed his arm.

Carl was extra careful after that but began to think that the police were watching him closely.

A week later when Carl got to work and went to pick up his tool box, the person who made the daily assignments consulted a special list he kept on his desk and told Carl that he was to report to room 124.

Carl walked to the room with trepidation. "Could they have caught up to me?" he wondered. "Maybe they've been watching me for months and that incident of the falling tool last week only tipped their hand. Now they feel they've got to act. Of course, it could just be that I'm being transferred and they'll just tell me that in room 124."

He reached the room and walked in. An individual dressed in the typical clothing of the managerial class was sitting at the only desk in the room.

"Ah, Reh Sans, please sit down," he said, gesturing towards a chair. The man continued working on the papers on his desk and said, "I'll be with you in a minute."

Carl felt a little relieved. The person seemed to be an official of relatively low rank assigned to paper work. He was probably just going to give Carl a new job assignment.

Presently the man gathered together the papers he had been working on and put them on the side of his desk. He picked up a folder and opened it and looked at Carl in a friendly way.

"Reh Sans, you have done very well on your assignments," he began. He glanced at a paper in the file and said, "The report on the generator you repaired at the sulfur processing plant is very favorable."

Picking up another sheet, he said, "You quickly determined the fault in the data link at the communications center."

The man put down the papers, folded his hands, and leaned back in his chair in a relaxed, congenial manner. "Tell me, Reh Sans, do you have a special interest in propulsion systems? On several occasions you were observed reading the blueprints of spaceship engines. Are you just interested in engines?"

Carl felt a constriction in his throat and shifted his weight in his chair slightly. He cleared his throat and said, "Well I've always been fascinated by spaceship engines." His palms were sweating.

"Have you?" answered the man. He reached forward and glanced at another paper in the folder. "Tell me, Reh Sans, does your interest extend to photographing schematics?" The friendliness had disappeared and an accusatory, challenging manner came over the man.

"I, ah . . . , sometimes photograph things so that I can study them more at leisure at home," Carl began.

"You could apply for the job of repairing spaceship engines if you are that interested," interrupted the man. Picking up another paper, he said, "You were also observed photographing the design plans of the central power station when you were assigned the job of repairing a circuit breaker at that facility."

The man pressed a button on his desk and said, "Your interest in photography intrigues me, Reh Sans."

Two armed guards entered the room almost immediately and Carl was escorted to the prison. Nancy was already there as they had picked her up soon after Carl had left for work.

Carl's interrogation lasted less than two hours. Nancy and Carl admitted how out of curiosity they has sneaked on board the spaceship and had failed to get off in time.

Nancy and Carl found when they got to prison that about a hundred other Californians had been caught over the years and were there too. They were kept in a large building that consisted of a number of small rooms and several large barrack like rooms. Nancy and Carl got a small room to themselves. There were no bars or cells but a tall wall surrounded the building and guards were posted in turrets along the wall. Carl found out that not only Californians but also Philadelphians, who were not dangerous, were prisoners in the building.

# Chapter 5

Carl and Nancy became good friends with George Erickson and Carol Chandler, who were engaged, and Janet Snyder and Gayle Poitiers, who were nurses. George Erickson's father owned a chain of restaurants in Los Angeles and Carol Chandler was a high school teacher. They had gotten to the planet about the same way Nancy and Carl had. They noticed the flying saucer and began snooping around. George and Carol had gone aboard the spaceship and couldn't get off in time just like Nancy and Carl.

Janet and Gayle had been spotted around the landing site. They were seized by the Philadelphians and taken on board the spaceship.

There was a Philadelphian, Ambar by name, in the room next door to Carl and Nancy. He was a political prisoner who had once been an official on the Philadelphian home planet. Carl had passed him a number of times in the exercise yard and also in the mess hall. One day he greeted him with a wave of his hand and a word of friendliness.

One day as Carl was returning to his room from the laundry room, he encountered Ambar in the upper hall way.

"Hello," said Carl.

"Good day, sir," answered Ambar. "Was the laundry room crowded?" he asked, noticing the basket of clean clothes in Carl's hands.

"No, there was just one other person in the laundry," replied Carl. After a pause, Carl ventured, "When do you suppose your people will be retuning to their home planet? They certainly have a lot of spaceships now."

He thought he might strike up a conversation and find out about the Philadelphians.

"It's hard to say. New Barstow is very strong. To find a chink in its armor will take close scrutiny and a lot of planning," replied Ambar.

Ambar was of medium size and had brown eyes. His white hair indicated that he was quite old. Ambar was a friendly person and continued, "I was put in here because

I differed with the authorities back home on the degree of arms buildup."

"You had those arguments also?" asked Carl in surprise.

"Oh, yes. The others—the other senators, I was a senator then—advocated an enormous arms buildup to hold off the encroaching Dynasty. I, on the other hand, argued for a diminished arms program. I felt that we did not need an invincible military machine but rather one that was just strong enough to convince the Dynasty that we would not surrender our sovereignty and could not be overcome without enormous and unacceptable losses on their part."

"Anyway the other senators were in the majority and we developed a gigantic military apparatus. The New Barstow colony, known as the Dynasty, had to counter it and brought a similar military system into our district."

"One day they made a maneuver in the sky that appeared to us to be an attack. Our forces responded in full force. In less than an hour our country became uninhabitable. We're the remnant that got away."

"So, why are you in this prison?" asked Carl. "Your view seems to have been correct."

"I have the habit of arguing against the prevailing view," said Ambar, grinning. "You see they are planning to go back and wrest a region away from the Dynasty for a home. I suggested—perhaps too strenuously—that we should seek a region far away from the New Barstow Dynasty's domain. I suggested that we use earth to equip ourselves and then depart to seek our new home."

"So that's why all these spaceships are being built," said Carl.

"Right, and it appears we are about ready to leave for the encounter," said Ambar.

Carl returned to Nancy and his quarters. After telling Nancy what Amber had said, Nancy said, "So they've been here for ten years, using our resources to outfit themselves for a return to their own solar system,"

"Yes, and Ambar thinks they're about ready to leave."

"I've been talking to the other people here from earth," said Nancy. "George and Carol decided to get married and they had a little ceremony with the other people from earth. There wasn't any clergy or judge to pronounce them married but they plan on getting properly married when they get back to earth—if we ever do."

"I wonder what will become of us when they leave to fight the Dynasty," said Carl.

"Do you suppose they will let us go? How would we get back to earth?" asked Nancy.

"I don't know. They might take us along rather than leave us behind to die. They seem to be decent enough people," said Carl.

"But if they take us along, how will we ever get back?" asked Nancy in an agitated voice.

In a few weeks, word came that they were all going to leave together. All of the prisoners from earth would be put in one of the cargo transport space ships, not a war ship.

The entire force would be put into a deep sleep for the four year trip to Alpha Centauri. Everyone was assigned a sleeping capsule that would be kept at a very cool temperature in order to slow down metabolism. Everything was controlled by a computer on board each spaceship.

The course of the armada through space was carefully calculated in order to escape detection by the Dynasty. Everybody would be awakened at least 30 days before our scheduled arrival at the battle site.

# Chapter 6

During the first week after they emerged from sleep, the hardest thing for Carl to adjust to was realizing that four years had elapsed since they left Saturn. It seemed unreal when Nancy and Carl and the others talked about it.

"Can we even see our sun as a star?" asked Nancy. "Which way do we look to find it?"

They all went over to the port hole shaped windows and peered out at the stars. Finally, George Erickson decided that he had found the sun. It was just a small star and everybody felt terribly lonely being that far from home.

Nancy was holding Carl's hand and sighing. "Do you think we'll ever get back? To consider dying out here is so depressing." She started to cry and Carl gave her a reassuring hug.

They could see the armada now as they were reflecting Alpha Centauri's light. The formation extended several miles across and occasionally the spaceships would change positions slightly. The earth prisoners assumed that the combat information center must be very busy and tense. Everyone wondered where the New Barstow, also known as the Dynasty, forces were and searched the sky for specks of light.

The next morning Carl was awakened by violent maneuvering of the ship. He was sure the battle had begun and wanted to get to the windows. Several others were awake also and soon they were all scanning the sky for signs of the enemy.

George called out, "There's one," and pointed to the upper right. Everyone looked and they could see a bright speck moving rapidly to the left. It made an abrupt stop and started getting larger.

"It's coning at us," gasped Nancy.

"I think you're right," somebody said.

Soon their cargo ship was maneuvering frantically in an attempt to evade the incoming spaceship. They turned to the right, putting the attacking Dynasty ship to their rear and accelerated rapidly. Nancy and Carol fell to the floor.

Carol helped Nancy up and said, "We don't have any weapons to fire at the incoming spaceship in our defense.

We had better find some sort of shelter or safe place. This old cargo ship might blow up."

Everybody was scurrying for some sort of cover.

"Shouldn't we have space suits on or be in some kind of escape shuttle if this thing gets hit?" asked George. "Maybe we would be picked up if we were in an escape shuttle out there. I mean if this cargo ship is destroyed and we get out on a space shuttle we might live through the battle."

"Maybe we ought to go to the control room of this ship and ask for escape directions," Carol said.

"They might not destroy a cargo ship," Carl said. "Maybe they'll just capture this thing."

Just then they were knocked to the floor by a sharp jolt.

"We're hit," somebody said.

They got up after a few moments and started moving forward towards the control room. When they passed a window they looked out.

"That's the Dynasty's ship." exclaimed Nancy and they were all standing gazing out at an enormous spaceship just outside.

They looked about and finally George said, "They're sending a boarding party aboard. Look!" he said, pointing.

They could see several figures moving from the Dynasty ship to the cargo ship.

"We had better hide," said Nancy. "Maybe they won't know about us or look for us."

Everybody frantically looked for a place of concealment. Some opened cargo boxes and climbed inside. Others scurried for small rooms along the passageway.

Carl and Nancy chose a room overlooking the command center to conceal themselves. The room was where the steward on duty sat. He had the task of providing the commander with the coffee like drink that the Philadelphians liked. The room had a small slit or shutter in one wall through which the steward used to watch the commander and his assistants for orders. There was a dumb waiter in one wall that Nancy and Carl could crouch in if necessary.

Carl watched as the Dynasty police entered the room. A short fusillade erupted during which two crew members were wounded and a Dynasty soldier was hit. The other Dynasty soldiers showed so little concern over their comrade's injury that Carl thought that perhaps the Dynasty police were robots.

Having subdued the other cargo ship crew members, the Dynasty soldiers just stood placidly at attention. This corroborated Carl's feeling that the Dynasty soldiers were robots.

"Nancy, watch these Dynasty soldiers. I think they are robots," said Carl.

"Why, what makes you think so?" asked Nancy looking through the shutter.

"Watch the placid, unemotional deportment of the Dynasty soldiers," said Carl. "They barely took notice of their comrade there on the floor when he was shot by a cargo ship crew member," said Carl.

"They're standing very still and at attention," said Nancy. "They are barely moving a muscle."

"Yes, their task is complete and they're awaiting new instructions," said Carl.

At that moment the door of the command center swung open and in stepped a Dynasty officer. He wore a green uniform with black helmet. Several uniformed Dynasty soldiers entered with him and took up positions around the room.

The Dynasty people were about the same size as the Philadelphians and of similar appearance. They just wore different uniforms and insignia.

"They look the same as the Philadelphians, of course," said Carl, "since they are descended from the same group of Europeans and Americans who left earth 130 years ago."

"I wonder if that's the boarding officer in charge," said Carl. He's in the command center which would be the logical destination for the boarding commander."

"What's he doing?"

"He's examining the ship's log right now," said Nancy peering through the shutter. "Now, he appears to be issuing commands to some of the others. They're scrambling about now, opening drawers and examining papers. One is leaving the room," said Nancy.

"Do you suppose those robots can sense our presence even if they can't see us?" asked Carl. "They might have heat seekers."

"I don't know but they will be coming this way eventually," said Nancy.

They heard something in the hall and immediately bounded for the dumb waiter. They climbed up the dumb waiter shaft and pulled the metal carriage behind them, keeping the metal carriage between themselves and the opening through which they entered. One of the Dynasty soldiers put his head into the shaft and looked up and down the shaft but apparently detected nothing.

When the soldiers left, Nancy and Carl carefully slipped down into the steward's room and went to the viewing slit again.

Carl looked through the slit. "They've evidently taken control of the ship," he said. "That boarding commander, or whatever he is, is sitting in the commander's seat and operating the controls."

They felt the ship moving.

"I wonder if the others were captured," said Nancy. "Where do you think they will take us?"

"We will soon find out. I suppose that they will take this ship to their local base or fortress," said Carl.

"I'm getting hungry," said Nancy. "Do you suppose we dare make our way back to our quarters?"

"OK, let's give it a try," answered Carl.

# Chapter 7

The trip to the Dynasty fortress was made at near light speed. Nancy and Carl determined that from watching the stretched out or streaked appearance of the stars when they looked out of the ship's port holes. Nancy and Carl spent several days searching through the ship for the other earth people. They looked for George, Carol, Janet, and Gayle but couldn't find them. They finally had to conclude that all the others had been captured and were being held as prisoners someplace near the command center.

Evidently the battle had been won by the Dynasty, or the Philadelphians had fled for the time being.

After several days Carl and Nancy noticed that they were slowing down and began watching for the Dynasty fortress.

"It must be that light up ahead," said Nancy one day when she was watching through a port hole. "That same light has been up ahead for a whole day now."

"I think you are right," replied Carl. "Is it close enough to tell anything yet?" he asked.

"No, but its getting bigger all the time," she answered.

The next morning when Nancy looked out the port hole the station was near enough to be seen clearly.

"Wow," said Nancy. "It's a huge planet like thing just floating in the sky."

"What does it look like?" asked Carl, excitedly. There was only one porthole in the part of the ship where they were and Nancy was looking through it.

"Well it's sort of an ellipsoid just sitting in space," she answered. "A structure protrudes downward and a smaller one extends upward," she added. "Its color is light yellow; or rather, its lights are yellow."

"How big is it?" asked Carl.

"I can't tell," she answered. "There is nothing around by which I can gauge its size. Wait, here come some spaceships that will be passing us and continuing on to the base." After a minute she said, "They are now approaching the base and they appear really small by comparison, just specks." She turned away from the port hole and looked at Carl.

Carl moved forward to look out the port hole.

"The station is huge," said Nancy with fear in her voice.

They continued to slow down and other spaceships hovered around to meet them.

"We are just going to have to disguise ourselves as Dynasty people this time," said Carl with a wry smile. "Before we disembark I want to get a printout of the flight path this cargo ship took to get to this base. We will need that to find our way back to the Titan moon of Saturn. From there we can stow away aboard the shuttle back to earth."

They decided to get into the base inside a cargo container again. They reasoned that the Dynasty was interested in the cargo or else they would have just let the cargo ship drift into some sun.

They climbed inside a container of lumber. Evidently everyone in this universe liked wood furniture. This lumber came from the forests of Oregon.

Late that night, after they had entered the base, they crept out of their container.

"We are getting pretty good at sneaking around," said Carl. "This is the second alien society we've crept about in."

Everywhere they looked they saw military equipment. It was clear that this was a military outpost on the frontier or border of the Dynasty's domain. Everyone was in uniform. There didn't seem to be any families, just everybody going about his duty. It was easy to tell the robots from the others. The robots just marched into a big building and were shut off.

The few remaining people scurried about doing whatever they had to do.

Nancy and Carl disguised themselves as soldiers and went on a tour.

"Look up there," said Carl. "Are those bars on those windows?"

"A jail," said Nancy. "I wonder how many people are in there. Do you suppose George and Carol or Janet and Gayle were caught and put in there?"

"Perhaps," said Carl.

They moved around the base, posing as soldiers on important assignments. The Dynasty people looked just like the Philadelphians and also like Nancy and Carl. In their uniforms and helmets, Nancy and Carl were able to pass without attracting attention.

Nancy and Carl found a vacant room down one of the out of the way passageways where they could live. The space station was so immense that it afforded many such places for concealment.

They picked up the few words they needed to communicate with the Dynasty people and stayed out of the recreation centers where their true identity might be noticed.

One day as Nancy was walking down one of the halls on the eighth floor she passed a person, who was evidently a servant. She nearly stopped him in his tracks because he was almost certainly a prisoner. She could hardly wait until she got home to tell Carl.

"I saw a prisoner today," she exclaimed as soon as she got in the door. "Maybe it was someone from our space ship," she said breathlessly.

"Where?" asked Carl.

"On the eighth floor in the administration complex or whatever they call it," she said. "He looked like a servant or something. He was wearing a costume that was not military in nature and he was carrying a tray with cups on it."

"What did he look like?" asked Carl.

"Oh, he was about 5 feet, 10 inches tall, maybe 35 years old, and had blond hair. He wore a light blue type of suit, not a military uniform."

It didn't surprise either of them any more that there were California prisoners on these planets or stations.

"We ought to get into that jail some day to find out who is in there," said Carl. "Maybe we will find our four friends from Saturn: George, Carol, Janet, and Gayle."

"Yes sure, and get caught in the process," responded Nancy.

"We would have to be very careful. But we ought to find out how many prisoners there are here," said Carl.

"Well maybe," said Nancy doubtfully. "But let's not do it just yet."

After a pause she continued, "Do you think we will ever get out of here? We don't even know where we are."

This was a distressing fact for both of them. They had traveled a long way after they left the battle scene at Alpha Centauri. They had approached nine tenths the speed of light in transit. This Dynasty space station where they were was near no sun and consequently was completely dark except for artificial light. They had located the map room in the headquarters part of the space station but hadn't had tine yet to figure out anything. The trouble was they couldn't stop or pause any place very long because they had to appear to be on some assignment or errand. Carl had recently located a camera and was determined to photograph the maps so that they could study them at their leisure.

During the next few weeks Carl managed to pass through the jail several times and finally discovered where the earth people were kept. There were about 100 of them and they were all kept in a wing on the fifth floor of the jail. Carl hadn't had a chance to talk to any of them and they didn't talk to their jail keepers. They just responded to gestures and jabs by their jailers.

"I bet they are new acquisitions," said Carl. "The Dynasty hasn't bothered to figure out their language or anything. The jailors just push them around."

"Should we speak to one?" asked Nancy.

After a pause Carl answered, "No, not just yet. They might say something, or rather, act in such a way that their jailors might suspect that we are earth people hiding in Dynasty uniforms. Let's examine the log books of all Dynasty spaceships for the last year or so; and maybe we can find out how the Dynasty captured these prisoners."

Everything had been entered on the station computers. The log books might be in some cabinet some place but the contents of the logs were on the station computer.

Carl and Nancy rigged a terminal on one of the computer's IO buses from materials they found in an electronics supply room. Over the following few weeks Nancy worked her way into the computer's files via the IO system and discovered the records about the Californians.

She found the record of the capture of the Philadelphian cargo ship that she and Carl had been on. The record indicated that the Dynasty found nearly 100 prisoners on board the Philadelphian space ship and put them in the jail on the Dynasty base.

The records showed that the Dynasty knew about the earth's sun and planet earth, of course, but apparently had little interest in earth or its people. The earth's sun was just entered as a star in their star atlas. There was also a record of several encounters between the Dynasty and pirate space ships manned by people from the various states in the New Barstow colony in Alpha Centauri.

"Do you suppose the pirates kept records?" asked Nancy.

"I doubt it," answered Carl. "They were just interested in commodities, not history and stuff like that. I suppose they know about a lot of different people from different places but for them that just provides interesting conversational material for use when they visit amongst themselves."

After a few minutes, Carl said, "Do you realize that if we erased the computer's memory of earth and destroyed the original ship's log books and got the Californians out of jail, that the Dynasty wouldn't even concern itself with the planet earth? They would just continue to ignore us in the future as they have in the past. They certainly must know that they came originally from earth."

"Earth must be way on the periphery of the Dynasty and they haven't paid any attention to us yet," said Carl.

"So what are you suggesting?" asked Nancy. "Are we going to spring those Californians from prison, wipe out the computers memory of us, and just take off in some spaceship?"

"Exactly!" said Carl.

# Chapter 8

A couple of weeks later Nancy went up to a Californian, who was out of jail for the day on some servant assignment. Her name was Deborah and she was from Cleveland, Ohio. At first Deborah thought Nancy was a Dynasty soldier and was amazed to find out Nancy was a Californian disguised as a Dynasty soldier and hiding out.

Before long, a command center was set up in a seldom entered portion of a warehouse. It was possible for Californian inmates of the jail to slip out of the jail and go to the command center since security at the jail was lax. However, it was deemed wise for them to return to the jail after short stays at the command center so that the jail population would not become noticeably altered.

One of the people who stayed in the warehouse command center on a regular basis was a former army officer from Virginia, Colonel Ralph Smith. Two other command post regulars were an aeronautical engineer from New York State, Charles Richardson, and an electrical engineer from Atlanta, Georgia, Albert Haynes. Various other people from the jail came for several days at a time as an escape plan developed. Dynasty uniforms were made for everybody at the command center; in fact, a uniform was made for everyone in jail.

Colonel Ralph Smith, Nancy, and Carl moved about freely during the day, mapping out a plan of attack. It was decided that the Californians would quietly and unobtrusively depart in a spaceship after destroying every record of their existence in the Dynasty's computers. The Dynasty, which was the central government of New Barstow, was in constant struggle with states in New Barstow and accordingly lost spaceships every once in a while.

Colonel Smith said there was a junk yard or scrap yard not far from the Dynasty jail where they dumped wrecked spaceships that were damaged in one of their battles. He thought it should be possible for us to rebuild one of these damaged spaceships for our use without being seen since the Dynasty paid little or no attention to this junk yard. There are plenty of spare parts lying around the junk yard to use in the repair. Charles Richardson thought that it might be possible to render the Dynasty's environment surveillance system temporarily inoperative by damaging some component in the surveillance system during the time that we attempted our escape. We Californians could steal away undetected in our refurbished spaceship.

Albert Haynes and Charles Richardson reconnoitered the large junk yard in search of a suitable damaged spaceship. They finally settled on one on the third day. It was going to take about four months to complete the overhaul and they would need to have several men from the jail working on it every day.

An important aspect of the entire plan was to leave no trace whatever of Californian presence on the base once we were gone. Except for the Californians in the jail, the Dynasty had little interest in earth or its inhabitants, and we wanted to keep it that way. Everything had to be timed just right on our departure.

While Charles Richardson and Albert Haynes were taking care of rebuilding the spaceship, Nancy and Carl began a systematic search through the Dynasty computer system for all references to the Californians in the jail.

All cross references were noted and ways were devised for removing this data from the computer when the time came for our departure. Several people from the jail, who were working at the command center, were delegated the job of finding the computer record of every spaceship that had come to the Dynasty post. If any of them had brought Californians to the port, then the plan was to delete from the ship's log any reference to the Californians.

Charles Richardson finally discovered a method for rendering the Dynasty's detection system non operational in one sector for about 14 minutes. He noticed from examining inventories that certain parts in the detection system burned out every year or so. If he caused a certain sequence of these parts to burn out simultaneously, the detection system would be inoperative for about a quarter of an hour. Since the burned out parts would be of the sort that frequently burn out, the Dynasty wouldn't become suspicious later on when reviewing the event.

The only really difficult problem was that some of the Californians had come into contact with the Dynasty people as slaves and perhaps the Dynasty people might remember them. Robots went to the jail to fetch the

Californians but that was no problem since the robot's memory would be erased. It was decided that these servants should be represented as jail inmates who had died; then the Dynasty people who had them as servants wouldn't think that anything was amiss when their servants didn't report to perform their duty.

The group planning the departure had to decide what portions of the station's computer records were to be modified. There were three levels of awareness of earth in the station's computer system. Firstly, there was the file of spaceship logs, where the records of first Californian contact by the spaceships were recorded. Secondly, there was the local station's file which is a fairly detailed record of Californian physiological parameters and also a record of Californian cultural attainment. Thirdly, there was a brief entry in the imperial report that was sent to Dynasty headquarters once every 20 days. It merely described Californian form, cultural attainment, and quality of the planet earth in brief form.

This third record had caused a lot of group discussion. The report had been sent to Dynasty headquarters and removing it here at the outpost would not obliterate it from headquarters' knowledge. The group discussed it at length and decided the only way out was to send an update report to headquarters that would discount or diminish the importance of earth to Dynasty ambitions.

"This will be a little tricky," Carl had said when everyone was discussing it at the meeting. "We will have to do it on the day that this station sends its usual report. Only, we will have to append our false data onto this station's communication message when it goes out without anyone in this station knowing it."

"How can we possibly do that," asked Colonel Smith.

"Well, can you get into the radio communications center, Charles, when they are sending the message?" asked Carl. "Then perhaps we can send our message at the end of the station message without anyone at the station detecting it."

"Possibly," answered Charles. "It sounds possible. I'll have to check it."

A few days later Charles Richardson reported that it was possible provided he had the message properly coded and ready to send at the conclusion of the station 20 day report. Accordingly, Nancy and Carl prepared the message after checking the usual code for such updates.

It was decided to put the plan in action about six months downstream, and to schedule it on a day when the station makes one of its 20 day reports to Dynasty headquarters. This put the day of departure near or on September 15th.

The most time consuming or labor intensive part of the project was the refurbishing of the spaceship that had been selected in the junk yard. Albert Haynes and Charles Richardson, who had chosen the spaceship, came every morning to the junk yard to direct the workers who had been sent from jail to work that day. Sometimes, Albert and Charles could assign the day's work to the men and then depart for other tasks.

Every morning Albert Haynes would greet the men, "Good morning gentlemen." They would respond, "Good morning, sir."

One morning Albert Haynes said, "I have been examining the radar and radio equipment on our ship. It looks like it was damaged in some long ago battle. We will have to hunt around in the junk yard for a better radar set and install it in our spaceship. Have any of you worked in radar or radio communications?"

One man answered, "I have. I worked on radars and radios in the air force."

Another man said, "I have also. I worked in the U S Weather Bureau."

"Good," said Albert. "Please come with me."

As they set off, Charles Richardson said to the others, "Let's complete the wok on the walls and floors of the second deck today, gentlemen."

One man asked, "Does the electric range work in that kitchen?"

Charles Richardson answered, "It looked OK when I inspected it a few days ago. We'll have to have electric power to test it though."

Another man said, "For electric power and engine thrust we will need to start up that nuclear reactor."

"That is correct," answered Charles Richardson. "Albert Haynes and I have been examining the engine and nuclear reactor. Fortunately, we found some instruction manuals in the shed inside warehouse 5."

"But where will we get the nuclear charge or reactor rods?" asked the man.

"Well, the nuclear reactor rods are stored in that building over there," said Charles Richardson, pointing to a building with sturdy looking walls. "There is a loading crane parked next to the building."

"But, for today, let's just finish the walls and floors of the second deck corridor," said Charles. "We can get to the kitchen later this week."

Four days later Charles Richardson started his crew on the mess hall.

"Good morning, men," said Charles Richardson, "Today we will start refurbishing the mess hall."

One of the men said, "I heard that we will be on this spaceship for four years."

"That's right," answered Charles Richardson.

"Well, if a hundred people are going to eat in this mess hall for four years," continued the man, "we are going to need a gigantic pantry to hold all the food."

"Also, a gigantic refrigeration room to hold all the perishable food," added another man.

"That won't be necessary," said Charles Richardson.

"Why is that?" asked the man.

We will be sleeping most of the four years," answered Charles Richardson.

"Do you mean we have to sleep in those sleep hibernation capsules again?" asked the man.

"Yes," answered Charles Richardson. "We will return to the Titan moon the same way we left it. We will use the sleep hibernation Capsules going both directions."

"When will we use the mess hall, then?" asked one worker.

"We will use the mess hall and kitchen for a number of days before we use the sleep hibernation capsules," said Charles Richardson, "and also for a number of days just prior to landing on Titan."

"Well, let's get going on the mess hall then," said a worker.

They took a tour of the mess hall that was on their spaceship.

"This room must have been struck by some kind of rocket in a battle long ago," said one man.

"Yes," answered Charles Richardson. "Several parts of the ship were destroyed in that battle."

"So, do we get replacement parts from some other spaceship in this junk yard?" asked the man.

"Yes," answered Charles Richardson. "Let's make a list of the replacement parts we need and then we will look through the other spaceships in the junk yards for those parts."

There were twenty tables with six chairs per table in the mess hall. Four of the tables were damaged.

"Not only will we have to replace those tables," said one worker, "but we will have to replace this wall as well where the rocket entered the spaceship."

After making their list, they set out in search of replacement parts.

"Let's try this spaceship," said one man, pointing to a spaceship in the junk yard. "It doesn't seem to be damaged too much."

"Albert Haynes and I checked out this spaceship," said Charles Richardson, "about a month ago. It wasn't damaged much in battle. We figure an engine was destroyed in battle, but not the rest of the ship."

"So, the mess hall should be in fine shape," said a worker.

"Yes, I think you're right," said Charles Richardson.

They entered the spaceship and proceeded to the mess hall. The mess hall was not damaged at all. They had no difficulty removing the parts they needed from the spaceship and carrying them to the spaceship that they were refurbishing for themselves. It took them only two days to replace the tables in their spaceship and repair the walls.

The next day Charles Richardson greeted his work crew and said that they would be working on the recreation room.

"Are we going to have a recreation room?" asked a worker.

"Yes," answered Charles Richardson. "People like to meet and talk to each other on trips."

"So, we will use this recreation room as a meeting hall before and after our long hibernation sleep," said one man.

"Yes," said Charles Richardson. "It is a good place for the captain to pass out orders to the passengers. Also, there are several days when we just have to travel a distance and it is nice to have some one to talk to."

"Let's examine the condition of the recreation room on our spaceship," said one worker.

"OK," said Charles Richardson.

They walked to the location of the recreation room.

"It doesn't look too bad," said one worker.

"Nothing is damaged," said another.

"Let's just leave it the way it is," suggested a worker.

"That's OK with me," said Charles Richardson.

"Our next task is to refurbish the sleep hibernation capsules in each cabin," said Charles Richardson.

"How can we determine if they are in working order?" asked one worker.

"Let's wait until tomorrow," said Charles Richardson, "when Albert Haynes will be here. We can work on the sleep hibernation capsules then."

The next day Charles Richardson and Albert Haynes met with the work crew.

"Good morning, gentlemen," said Albert Haynes.

"Good morning," returned the men.

"The sleep hibernation capsules present us with a challenge," began Albert Haynes.

"Do we have any manuals or instructions for the capsules?" asked one worker.

"Yes, we do," answered Albert Haynes. "Charles Richardson and I have found several manuals that describe the sleeping capsules."

"Where are they?" asked the worker.

"They are in building 5," answered Albert Haynes.

"We will go over and get them in a few minutes," said Charles Richardson.

"But, we must also find an electric power source to use in testing them," said Albert Haynes.

"We were looking through the manuals the other day," said Charles Richardson, "and there were a lot of standard test procedures to ensure that the sleeping capsules are working correctly. But, an electric power source is necessary to conduct the tests."

"Maybe we can find a battery cart in that building 5 that we could use," said one worker.

"Yes," said Charles Richardson.

"Let's go over there now," said Albert Haynes, "and get the manuals and look for a battery cart."

They walked to building 5. It was a large building that contained a lot of tools and various manuals.

"Here are the manuals for the sleep capsules," said Albert Haynes, pointing to a large book case. "Let's take them down and put them on that push cart over there."

The working crew put all the relevant manuals on the push cart.

"Now, we have to find a battery cart," said Albert Haynes.

"That shouldn't be too hard," said Charles Richardson. "The Dynasty keeps its tools in this building. They must have some batteries here."

After scouting the building for a while they located the battery room.

"Let's check the manuals and find out what kind of batteries we need," said Charles Richardson.

"This manual says we need a 12 volt battery capable of delivering one ampere," said one worker.

"Here is one of them," said Albert Haynes. "Let's take it. We can use the cart that we put the manuals on."

The crew took the manuals and the battery back to their spaceship.

"You know," said Albert Haynes, "we need oxygen for breathing as well. I suppose oxygen air hoses lead from the sleep capsules to a device somewhere in the space ship for removing the carbon dioxide from the exhaled air and restoring the oxygen content to its normal level before sending it back to the sleep capsules. However, to test the sleep capsules, we will probably need a tank of oxygen. That will also be mentioned in the test procedures in the manuals."

"Well, let's go back to building 5 and get the oxygen, then," said one worker.

Charles Richardson and one worker went back to building 5 and after searching through the building they finally found the room where the oxygen was stored in metal containers. They took one container and returned to their spaceship.

"Let's just go to one of the cabins and conduct the tests," said Albert Haynes.

"Here's cabin 10," said one of the workers.

"OK, let's use this one," said Albert Haynes.

They all went into the cabin, taking their manuals, battery power cart, and canister of oxygen.

"This is all a mystery to me," said one of the workers.

"Right," said Albert Haynes. "This is new to all of us. But we just have to follow the manuals very closely."

"We will do exactly what the manuals specify," said Charles Richardson.

"Well, let's begin with step one here on page seven," said Albert Haynes.

"It says, 'connect the battery to terminals marked + and – in the circuit box at the foot of the sleeping capsule,'" read Charles Richardson.

"Here is the circuit box," said Albert Haynes.

"OK, I'll connect the battery cable," said one of the workers.

"Red and green indicator lights just came on inside the capsule," said a worker.

"The next thing the manual says," said Albert Haynes, "is 'connect the oxygen canister hose to the pipe marked breathing oxygen at the foot of the sleeping capsule.'"

"Here is the pipe," remarked one of the workers.

They connected up the oxygen hose to the pipe.

"OK," said Albert Haynes. "We have connected the electric battery power and the oxygen for breathing to the sleeping capsule. Step 3 says 'Set Test Control to 5'. Do you see a control labeled Test Control?"

"Here it is," said Charles Richardson. "OK, I have set it to 5."

"There should be a button there," said Albert Haynes, "labeled Test Button."

"Got it," said Charles Richardson.

"Press it," said Albert Haynes.

"OK," said Charles Richardson.

"The meter, labeled Test Meter should read between 8 and 10," said Albert Haynes.

"It reads a little over 8," said a worker.

"OK," said Albert Haynes. "Step 4 says set the Test Control to 6."

"All right, I have set it to 6," said Charles Richardson.

"There should be a button labeled Ready up inside the capsule where the sleeper will lie down," said Albert Haynes.

"I found it," said a worker.

"All right," said Albert Hayes. "Step 5 says press the Ready Button, and check if oxygen enters the sleeping capsule from a vent near the lid."

"I am pressing the Ready Button," said Charles Richardson.

"Oxygen is coming from the vent in the sleeping capsule," said a worker.

"OK," said Albert Haynes. "I guess we have checked the breathing gas and it works OK."

"How many steps are there in the manual?" asked a worker.

Albert Haynes looked forward through the manual, and said, "There are 75 steps all together. We still have a ways to go."

"All right, let's go onto step 6," said Charles Richardson.

"Step 6," said Albert Haynes, "Set the Test Control to 7."

"All right, I set the Test Control to 7," said Charles Richardson.

"Press the Test Button," said Albert Haynes. "The meter on the circuit box should read between 12 and 15."

"It reads 14," said one of the workers.

They continued in this manner through all 75 steps.

"We are now at step 73," said Albert Haynes.

"Wait a minute," said Charles Richardson.

"What is it?" asked Albert Haynes.

"I just have to change my position," said Charles Richardson. "I am getting a cramp in my leg."

"Yes," said a worker, "I have had a cramp developing in my leg for a while."

"We have been at this checking procedure for nearly three hours," said Albert Haynes. "Maybe we should take a short break."

"I agree," said one of the workers."

They took a ten minute break during which time everyone gave a sigh of relief.

"OK," said Albert Haynes. "Let's finish this procedure so we can stop work for today."

"Step 73," announced Albert Haynes. "Set the Test Control to 85."

"Done," said Charles Richardson.

"Press the Test Button," said Albert Haynes.

They heard pleasant soft music coming through speakers in the sleeping capsule.

"I suppose that is the wake up alarm," said Charles Richardson.

"Step 74," said Albert Haynes. "Set the Test Control to 86."

"I just set it to 86," said Charles Richardson.

"Press the Test Button," said Albert Haynes.

"I just pressed the Test Button," said one of the workers.

The glass lid clasp clicked and the glass lid opened over the sleeping capsule.

"Step 75," said Albert Haynes. "Set the Test Control to 87."

"I just set it to 87," said Charles Richardson.

"Press the Test Button," said Albert Haynes.

"I pressed the Test Button," said a worker.

A voice message came over the speaker in the sleeping capsule announcing, "Your sleep hibernation is complete. You can arise and await directions from the spaceship commander."

"Well, everything checks out OK in the sleep capsule," said Albert Haynes.

"That is great," exclaimed one of the crew workers.

The work of refurbishing the spaceship proceeded in this manner day after day. After a little more than four months the job was completed and the spaceship passed all tests.

# Chapter 9

September 14<sup>th</sup> had been a day where things had been carried out at a near feverish pitch. Nancy and Carl awoke early on September 15<sup>th</sup>; they had had little or no rest the night before.

"Well, today's the big day," said Nancy excitedly.

"Yes, everything had better go right," returned Carl. "I suppose everybody is getting up now and thinking about his or her one assignment."

Colonel Smith and Albert Haynes had spent the night aboard the spaceship and Charles Richardson was packing his tool kit to take over to the surveillance system building where he would render the detection system inoperative for 14 minutes. Then Charles would head over to the radio communications center to append our message to the station's 20 day report.

Nancy and Carl entered the little side door at the rear of the computer building where they had been entering all along, The door was near the roadway and there was quite a bit of shrubbery around. It opened into a hallway in the basement that was not often used. They hurried to a small room that contained the telephone communication switch boxes for the building. They had in a previous week found that the computer data cables also passed down the same conduits between the floors and walls that the phone cables did. Consequently they had tapped into the computer cables and spent two weeks figuring out the protection codes to the computer memory banks. They then dumped the memory contents onto a disc they could take back to their room and analyze the data at their leisure. They kept a small keyboard and a silent electrostatic printer in an empty space in one wall where they lived.

They quietly entered the room with the telephone communication switch boxes now and locked the door behind them. "Let's open the switch box and get to the computer cables quickly," Nancy said. "We have got a lot to do."

"Right," responded Carl as he pried open the communication switch box and took his handheld computer and notebook from his pocket.

"I hope Charles Richardson is not having trouble up in the radio communications center appending our message to the station's 20 day report," said Nancy.

"He was pretty confident that he would succeed," replied Carl.

"I will patch into the computer I/O bus now and establish memory access," said Nancy while attaching leads from Carl's computer to the computer I/O bus. "What are those access codes again?"

"Here. We have them in our little notebook," said Carl, pointing to a long number in a spiral notebook he held in his hand. "It's the access number we figured out to gain access to the portion of their computer memory that contains information about earth."

Nancy entered the access code and established memory access. "I'm ready now to start deleting the references to earth Californians," said Nancy.

Carl said, "All right, here is the first set of values to enter."

Nancy proceeded to type in the numbers and characters that erased the station's memory of earth Californians. They were finished in about 10 minutes.

"OK, let's put this computer equipment in our bag and get out of here," said Carl. They put their equipment in their bag and proceeded to leave the building. They turned left upon leaving the building and headed towards the spaceship launch pad.

"I wonder if everything went smoothly with everybody else," said Nancy;

"Well if it didn't we'll soon know," replied Carl.

They chose a path that would take them by a trash dump so that they could dispose of their computer equipment in passing. Then they headed directly for launch pad 79 where the spaceship was located. They noticed a few others heading that way and assumed that they were other Californians.

"Colonel Smith said he would put a green cloth in the aft cabin door if everything was ready," Carl reminded Nancy. "Do you see it yet?"

"No," replied Nancy. "Where should we wait until it appears?"

"He said a day ago that there is a partly empty hanger just behind the spaceship where we can wait if he and Albert Haynes aren't ready when we all arrive."

"It must be that building with the number 18 on it," Nancy said.

"Yes, let's go there until the green cloth appears," said Carl.

When they got there, quite a few others were already waiting around.

"What do you suppose is holding up Colonel Smith; the green flag hasn't been displayed yet?" asked one of the people when Carl and Nancy entered the hanger.

"I don't know," answered Carl, looking at his watch. "Is everybody here?"

"Only Richardson hasn't arrived yet," answered one of the others.

"I wonder if he had trouble at the communication center," said Nancy in a worried voice. "Do you think so?"

"I hope not," said Carl looking at the hanger door.

Just then the green cloth appeared in the spaceship's cabin door.

"The green cloth's out," said Carl with relief.

"Great, let's get going," came from someone in the group.

As they hurried across the landing pad, Carl noticed Richardson hurrying along the side of one of the buildings. "Here comes Richardson," he said.

"Good," exclaimed Nancy.

They hurried up the gangway to the cabin door, Richardson scurrying to catch up, and entered the spaceship.

Colonel Smith and Haynes were at the controls operating switches. After we were all in the spaceship, Colonel Smith closed and secured the cabin door behind him. A minute later, we heard the engines roar to life!

They could feel the ship moving along the launch pad and everyone became tense. There was always the chance that some fighter pursuit spaceship would be up and challenge us.

"Did you succeed in defeating the detection equipment in the surveillance system building?" Colonel Smith asked Richardson.

"Yes, we have about 20 minutes before they diagnose the failure and replace the part," he answered. "We had better be far away by then."

"We will be long gone by then," said Colonel Smith with a grin as he gave the spaceship full throttle for take off.

They all felt the acceleration and let out a whoop of joy as they left the Dynasty space station. In about eight minutes they were traveling at about one twentieth the speed of light.

"They will never catch us now," yelled Colonel Ralph Smith with a look of great pleasure on his face.

# Chapter 10

"Well, thankfully we have escaped the Dynasty," said Charles Richardson, "but we have a long way to go. We have to go into four years of sleep hibernation on this spaceship before we reach the Philadelphian colony on Titan. Then we still have to get from Titan to Earth."

"How confident are you, Albert, that this sleep equipment is going to work correctly?" asked Nancy.

"I am very confident," answered Albert Haynes. "Charles Richardson and I have been testing and repairing this spaceship, including the sleeping equipment, for the past four months. We've renovated everything on board this spaceship."

"What will be our wake-up procedure prior to reaching Titan?" asked Carl.

Colonel Smith said, "Charles and I have calculated the flight time, and we think the wake-up alarm should occur ten days prior to our arrival."

"We've based our flight time calculations on this map we got from the Dynasty computer records," said Charles.

"We are very certain that we have read the map correctly," said Colonel Smith.

"I guess it is going to depend on the reliability of our spaceship," Carl said.

"Oh, the spaceship is in excellent condition," said Charles Richardson. "We can rely on her."

"Have you got all the reactor fuel rods that you need for the entire trip?" asked Carl.

"Yes, we have plenty of fuel rods for the reactor," answered Albert Haynes.

"What are the chances of a Philadelphian long distance reconnaissance spaceship spotting us while we are still asleep?" asked Nancy. "We won't be ready for such an encounter at all."

"We do have on board a radar system that can detect spaceships approaching us," said Albert Haynes.

Charles Richardson said, "Our plan is to have the computer slow us down from nine tenths the speed of light to 30,000 miles per hour before awakening us or turning on the radar."

Albert Haynes said, "If we have our computer system turn the radar on before we are awake then the Philadelphians might detect our radar scans."

"We ought to very carefully discuss this matter," said Carl. "We don't want to announce our presence by turning on our radar when we are still asleep. A Philadelphian reconnaissance cruiser might spot us and come aboard."

"We could wake up thirty days out," said Nancy, "and get well organized."

"So, what is the situation?" asked Carl. "Is it the case that they can't detect us when we are approaching at nine tenths the speed of light? But once we slow down we are detectable. Should the tactic then be to have the computer wake us up as soon as we slow down?"

"Yes, that is pretty much the tactic we are using," said Colonel Smith.

Albert Haynes said, "When we slow down from nine tenths the speed of light and everybody wakes up, we would be traveling at about 30,000 miles per hour."

"So, if we give ourselves only ten days of wakefulness before reaching Titan, we would be about 7 million miles from Titan when we wakeup," said Nancy. "That would be about twenty-eight times the distance from the earth to its moon. I suppose that is far enough away from Titan when we first decide to wake up."

"We brought only ten days supply of food aboard," said Colonel Smith. "If we wake up twenty or thirty days before reaching Titan, we will have to go on a diet."

"Well, 7 million miles from Titan is pretty close," said Carl. "The Philadelphian reconnaissance spaceships might patrol further out than that."

Colonel Smith said, "If we slow down and thereby become visible to the Philadelphians when ten days out, then they have only ten days to spot us. However, if we slow down when thirty days out, they will have thirty days to spot us. I think we are ahead with the ten day scenario."

"I concur," said Albert Haynes. "If we wake up when ten days out and turn on the radars after that, we will have our best chance."

"I guess you're right," said Carl. "What do you think, Nancy?"

"Well, OK, I guess that is best," answered Nancy.

"I agree," said Charles Richardson.

Carl said to Nancy, "Let's check our quarters on board this ship. We can look at our cabin and the sleep hibernation equipment."

"OK," said Nancy.

They left the cabin and proceeded to the living quarters of the one hundred Californians.

"My, this spaceship is huge inside," said Nancy.

"Yes. Albert Haynes and Charles Richardson along with help from many of the prisoners did a splendid job during the last four months," said Carl.

"I guess this light gray color of the walls and ceiling is the typical color of Barstonian spaceships," said Nancy. "That's why they could find so much of it in the junk yard."

"This tough dark floor carpet reminds me of what we use back home in public buildings," said Nancy.

"There must be several floors to this spaceship with stair cases between them," Carl said.

"Let's see, there are one hundred people. So, I suppose they made about fifty or sixty cabins," Nancy said.

"There are probably a dining hall and a recreation room as well," Carl suggested.

"I count twenty four cabins on this floor," said Nancy.

"Let's go down the stair case up ahead and look at the other floors," said Carl.

"We could check out the dining hall and then go to the recreation room and talk to the other passengers," said Nancy.

Carl tapped on the walls as he went along and said, "The material that the walls are made of must be strong, but very light. I wonder what it is. Do you suppose it is an aluminum alloy? It's hard to know what materials the Dynasty could mine from their planet."

"I don't know what it is," said Nancy.

When they got to the second floor, Carl asked, "What cabin number was assigned to us?"

"They gave us cabin 17," said Nancy. "That would be on the first floor."

"Why don't we look at the dining hall and talk with the other passengers before we look at our cabin?" asked Carl.

"OK," said Nancy.

They went down to the first floor and looked for direction signs. The signs consisted of light fixtures embedded in the wall. The words giving the direction were frosted onto the glass plates in front of the light bulb.

"I wonder how Albert Haynes managed to get all these signs made with English words," said Carl.

"He must have found some fancy tools and equipment to work with out there in the junk yard," replied Nancy.

"There's our direction sign," said Carl, pointing to a sign saying mess hall.

They proceeded down the hall, following the sign's directions, and passed the kitchen on their left.

"My, my, how elegant," exclaimed Nancy. "Look at all that bright modern equipment. The room is spacious and utilitarian. Notice all the table tops or work surfaces near the stoves and washing machines."

"Yes, very nice," said Carl.

"I wonder where the 10 day supply of food for a hundred people is being kept," said Nancy.

"In freezers, I suppose," answered Carl. "Just imagine the amount of electric power it takes to keep it frozen for 4 years."

"These spaceships must have some very high tech engines to achieve that," answered Nancy.

"Yes, but remember our aircraft carriers can stay out on the ocean for a year on nuclear reactor power plants that operate the engines as well as all of the ship's services," remarked Carl.

"Well, let's take a look at the dining hall, or mess hall," said Nancy.

"OK," responded Carl.

They continued down the hall until they came to the mess hall. They counted 20 tables with 6 seats per table.

"Very nicely decorated," exclaimed Nancy. "Look at those beautiful murals on the walls."

"I wonder where Albert Haynes and his workers found those?" asked Carl. "I suppose he got them from the Barstonian computer records; they must be photographs of New Barstow scenery."

"Let's continue on to the recreation room," said Nancy, "and chat with the folks."

Passing through the mess hall they came to the recreation room.

"Lovely," said Nancy. "Look at all the easy chairs upholstered in some kind of plastic foam. Beige furniture and walls, medium blue rugs and light blue ceiling. And, there are more murals on the walls."

"I see George and Carol," said Carl. "Also, Janet and Gayle. Let's ask them how their escape from prison was managed."

"Hi, everybody," said Nancy.

"Oh Hi, you two," returned Carol.

"How did all of you people get out of prison back at the Dynasty base without any alarm being sounded?" asked Carl.

"I think they drugged the guards," said George.

"I suppose so," returned Carl.

"We will have to affect a secret landing on Titan when we arrive there, and go into hiding for a while," said Nancy.

"Yes, the plan calls for a secret landing on Titan," said Carl, "and then we will have to stow away aboard shuttle spaceships for a trip to earth."

"What I would like to know is when we have to go into those sleep capsules," said Carol, "and when we wake up again. I hate those things."

"Me too," chimed in Janet.

"It's scary," said Gayle. "The hardest thing in the world is to close that capsule lid and breathe in the oxygen."

"I can't really get my self to trust the people who built them," said Carol.

"But we don't have any choice," said George.

"And, if you are the only one who won't close the lid and take the breath," said Carl, "you will soon be walking around in a very cold spaceship with a rapidly diminishing oxygen supply for four years."

"How gruesome a thought," put in Janet.

"Anyway, I suppose we have a couple of days before we have to take that step," said George.

"How many days did you say we would be awake on the other end before landing?" asked Carol.

"Right now, it looks like it is going to be ten days," answered Carl.

"Why such a short time?" asked Carol.

"We have only a ten day supply of food aboard," answered Nancy.

"Oh," responded Carol.

"So, what are we to expect during those last ten days?" asked George.

"Well, we will have 7 million miles to travel and the Philadelphians will almost certainly have reconnaissance spaceships up," answered Carl.

"Do we have any guns or rockets aboard to defend ourselves?" asked George.

"Albert Haynes might have put one machine gun or rocket launcher on board. I don't know. I doubt the Dynasty left any guns in their junk yard," answered Carl.

"So, if we are seen we will probably be boarded and put back in prison," moaned Nancy.

"I am afraid so," returned George.

"The main thing is to spend as little time as possible in a visible state," said Carl. "We are only visible after we return from nine tenths the speed of light to slow speed."

"Maybe we shouldn't come out of nine tenths the speed of light until we are just five days out from Titan," said Gayle.

"Well, that's certainly a thought," returned George.

"That would be cutting it a little close," said Carl. "We would have to take a pretty good aim, or we would miss Titan and slam into Saturn."

"Or crash into Titan," said George.

"If we can remain undetected for the ten days we will be all right," said Nancy. "Suppose we keep the radar and all other electro magnetic radiation off for ten days?"

"Or, approach Titan from an angle the Philadelphians aren't watching," said Gayle.

"You mean from a sector that the Philadelphians wouldn't expect an approach?" asked Carl.

"Yes, like an approach from the direction of Saturn," said Gayle.

"That would take a lot of engine power. We would have to avoid being drawn into Saturn," said Carl.

"I'll bring it up with Colonel Smith. He's flying this thing," said Carl.

Nancy and Carl returned to their cabin to examine their accommodations.

"So, we've got about ten feet by twelve feet of space," said Carl upon entering.

"Light green walls and white ceiling and brown rugs," said Nancy. "It matches the pale, soft tones in the other parts of the spaceship."

"It would be nice to have some bright reds and yellows and purple around," said Carl. "But Albert Haynes and his work crew of prisoners had more important things to do than devise a pleasant décor."

"We can sit on these brown sofas and talk and read if we can find some books," said Nancy.

"These two beds look comfortable," said Carl. "They become the sleeping capsules where we hibernate for four years when we pull down the glass covers and operate these controls."

"They look like the same capsules that were in the cargo ship when we came out," said Nancy.

"I can certainly sympathize with Carol when she says that she has a hard time psychologically when she has to pull the glass cover closed and breathe in the gas," said Carl.

"Should we go up to the pilot cabin and discuss with Colonel Smith and the others the best approach to Titan?" asked Nancy.

"Yes, we can tell them about our talk with the others in the recreation room," said Carl.

They left their cabin and went up the stairs to the third floor and then went forward to the pilot cabin.

"How big or long is this spaceship?" asked Nancy. "Did Albert Haynes or Charles Richardson say?"

"I think he said that it is about 400 feet long and about 40 feet in diameter," answered Carl. "The back or aft 100 feet are devoted to the nuclear reactors and engines and also the electric power generator."

"I guess the radioactive rods or pile, what ever it is called, will last the entire 4 year period," said Nancy.

"No doubt Albert Haynes and Charles Richardson got all the necessary information and requirements from the manuals that belonged to this spaceship before it was consigned to the junk yard," replied Carl.

When they reached the pilots cabin, they knocked on the door and went in. The cabin was very spacious; it went across the entire front of the ship. The pilot and copilot chairs looked very comfortable. The chairs were surrounded by dials and controls and were in a position that would provide good visibility for the pilot and copilot. The onboard computer was against the back wall.

"Hello, Colonel," said Nancy. "We just took a tour of the spaceship."

"Hello Nancy and Carl," responded Colonel Smith.

"We found the other Californians in the recreation room," said Carl.

"How do they like our great adventure?" asked Charles Richardson.

"Oh, they are of course thrilled," answered Carl. "But they are apprehensive about a number of things."

"What are they worried about?" asked Colonel Smith.

"Several things," chimed in Nancy. "They find the sleep capsules daunting for one thing. Another big concern is whether or not we will be attacked by the Philadelphians when we approach Titan."

"The sleep hibernation capsules will work just fine," said Albert Haynes. "The approach to Titan and a possible encounter with the Philadelphians could present some serious difficulties."

"We talked about how many days we should be awake before landing," said Nancy.

"The thought was advanced that the fewer days, the better," said Carl. "The Philadelphians are less likely to detect us if we are there a few days rather than many."

"Plus, we don't have any guns with which to protect ourselves," added Nancy.

"We have one small rocket launcher," said Albert Haynes. "We couldn't find any other guns in the junk yard."

"Somebody suggested that since the Philadelphians can't see us until we slow down, we should only slow down and wake up five days before landing," said Carl.

"How accurate are our computers and navigation maps?" asked Carl. "If we try to get within five days of landing before slowing down, might we not overshoot or crash into Titan?"

"Well, that is always a possibility," answered Charles Richardson.

"We won't have any course corrections while we are asleep," said Colonel Smith. "So, it all depends on how accurate our original aim is. As you know, that aim will be taken 4 years before our arrival at Titan."

"What if we wake up ten days before arrival but put the wake up location on the opposite side of Saturn from Titan?" asked Carl. "That way, they probably won't notice us arriving in their area."

"And then approach Titan from the Saturn side," said Colonel Smith. "With Saturn as a backdrop behind us, the Philadelphians would have a harder time spotting us."

"Saturn might appear as a slightly mottled or blotchy backdrop," added Charles Richardson. "They would have some difficulty separating us from the mottled background."

"Sounds like a good idea," said Colonel Smith.

"There is the danger of getting too close to Saturn before approaching Titan," mentioned Carl. "If we get too close to Saturn our engines might not be strong enough to keep us from being drawn into Saturn. Remember this spaceship was designed to lift off from a smaller planet than Saturn and therefore doesn't have very strong engines for its weight."

"I will check it using our computer data base and physics equations," said Albert Haynes.

"We ought to be able to calculate a flight path that approaches Titan from the direction of Saturn, given our mass and engine thrust." said Charles Richardson.

"OK, gentlemen," said Albert Haynes, "if you will step over to our computer screen you can see the envelope of possible paths given our ship's capabilities."

They all crowded around Albert and looked over his shoulder at the screen.

"The portion of a very large ball that you see there on the left is Saturn," said Albert Haynes. "The small ball on the right is Titan."

"I suppose the fan shaped figure between them is the envelope of all possible flight paths to Titan," said Colonel Smith.

"That's correct," said Haynes. "If you fly the edge of the fan nearest Saturn, you have to fly the fastest and burn the most fuel."

"And, if you fly the edge of the fan farthest from Saturn you fly the slowest and burn the least fuel," ventured Carl.

"Exactly," responded Albert Haynes.

"And all other flight paths through the fan require intermediate speeds," said Colonel Smith.

"I think what you have been discussing is our best plan," said Charles Richardson. "We should slow down from nine tenths the speed of light speed on the opposite side of Saturn from Titan and then spend ten days going around Saturn to approach Titan."

"And then use an approach to Titan on a flight path that lies inside your fan envelope, Albert," said Colonel Smith.

"Yes, I agree," said Albert Haynes.

"Me too," said Charles Richardson.

"What do you think, Carl?" asked Colonel Smith.

"I concur," said Carl.

"One of the big advantages of this plan," said Nancy, "is that we come out of near light speed ten days before we arrive. We don't have to aim as unerringly that way as we would if we come out of light speed while five days out."

"Right," said Albert Haynes.

"Everyone seems to be in agreement then," said Colonel Smith. "Albert Haynes, please calculate a flight path for us that will place us on Titan's orbit about Saturn, but on the opposite side of Saturn from Titan, and then store it in the computer's flight path record. Also store the command that will bring us out of near light speed just prior to reaching that point. Then calculate a path for us around Saturn that will allow us to approach Titan from the direction of Saturn using your fan envelope that we talked about before. When both paths and the command to slow down from near light speed have been calculated and stored in the computer, let me know."

"Yes sir," said Albert Haynes.

While Albert Haynes was busy on that assignment the others discussed the preparation of the passengers for the four year trip at nine tenths the speed of light.

"It will probably take us several days to accelerate from our current speed to nine tenths the speed of light," said Charles Richardson.

"We could all probably just move about during that time between our cabins and the recreation room and take our meals in the mess hall," said Nancy.

"Yes, I think you're right," responded Carl.

"People have to get themselves ready psychologically for climbing into their sleeping capsules—and closing the glass lid—a few days from now," said Nancy.

"Everybody did it before as a prisoner on that cargo spaceship a year ago," said Colonel Smith.

"One nice thing about coming out of near light speed on the far side of Saturn," said Charles Richardson, "is that the Philadelphians won't be looking for anybody there and consequently we won't come under attack the day after we slow down."

"Right, we won't be in a state of near panic on the first day we wake up," said Carl.

Albert Haynes said, "I have made the calculations, Colonel Smith, and they are stored in the computer's memory."

"OK," said Colonel Smith, "I will make the announcement over the ship's speaker system right after dinner tonight."

Nancy and Carl left the pilot cabin and returned to their cabin.

"My, it is an odd feeling to consider that in a few days we are going to go into a sleep for four years and wake up an enormous distance from here," said Nancy.

"Yes, but it sure will be nice to get home again," said Carl with a grin.

After dinner that night while the passengers were still in the mess hall or in the recreation room the Colonel's voice came over the speaker system to announce that the spaceship's flight path to Titan had been calculated and put into the ship's computer. He said that everyone should plan to enter his or her sleeping capsule at 9pm on Friday, close the glass lid, and press the Ready button.

"When you wake up," said Colonel Smith, "we will be orbiting Saturn and preparing for our approach to Titan."

George and Carol as well as Janet and Gayle were sitting at Nancy and Carl's table in the mess hall.

"I am glad we are proceeding with this," said Gayle. "A year ago, I thought we might never get home."

"Yes, it is scary but I am glad we are proceeding," said Janet.

"Well, we have a few days to relax and talk to each other before we have to use the sleep capsules," said Nancy.

"Yes, that's comforting," said Janet.

Two days later, Carl and Nancy were in their sleeping capsules in their cabin and it was approaching 9pm.

"I brought along my New Testament Scriptures," said Carl, "and I have been reading it. Do you have your Bible?"

"I have mine and I have also been reading it," said Nancy. "Make sure you say a prayer."

# Chapter 11

The melody was very pleasant. "It sounds familiar," thought Carl. "What is the name of it? It has something to do with hills and trees. There is a great white space out there now, with a glass door in front of it. Is that Nancy looking at me?"

Nancy was leaning over Carl's sleeping capsule. She smiled when she saw his eyes open. "Good morning, Carl. Very nice alarm system, isn't it?"

"As soon as you're up, you can take a look at Saturn," continued Nancy. "It is so near it dominates the entire window. Saturn is not very colorful, but it certainly is huge."

Carl sat up on his sleeping capsule with his legs dangling over the side. "I've got to wait for my metabolic rate to rise before I charge into the day," said Carl. "How long have you been up?"

"Oh, about an hour," said Nancy.

"Have you looked out into the hall or mess hall?" asked Carl. "Are many people up and around?"

"A few," said Nancy. "I glanced down the hall."

"So, ten more days and we are supposed to land on Titan," said Carl.

"Since Titan is on the other side of Saturn, we can't see it yet," said Nancy.

"I wonder if there is some kind of schedule for this first day's activities," said Carl.

"I imagine Colonel Smith, Albert Haynes, and Charles Richardson will call us all into the recreation room later today and describe our current situation," said Nancy.

"It would be nice if they could present a pictorial display of the flight path we will take from here to Titan," said Carl.

"Yes, we are to approach Titan from the direction of Saturn," said Nancy.

"Should we go up to the pilot's cabin to make sure everybody came out of their sleep hibernation all right?" asked Carl.

"OK," answered Nancy. "Are you at all hungry?"

"No. I think I'll just get one of those small bottles of water for now."

Nancy and Carl left their cabin on the first floor and proceeded down the hall to the stair case to the third floor. Gayle stepped out of her cabin into the hall up ahead.

"Hi, Gayle, how are you?" asked Nancy.

"Oh, Hi Nancy," returned Gayle. "I'm fine, I guess. I was just going to Janet's cabin to see how she is getting along."

"The return to slow speed and wake up went perfect," said Carl. "Everything seems to be great. Saturn is out there and very prominent."

"Yes it is," exclaimed Gayle. "The arrival at our destination and the wake up went very smoothly."

"We can't see Titan yet," said Nancy. "It's on the opposite side of Saturn. Carl and I are just going to the pilot's cabin to inquire about our rendezvous with Titan."

"OK," said Gayle. "Well, here is Janet's cabin. I'll just knock and see how she is."

"All right," said Carl. "We will see you in the mess hall later. By the way, are you at all hungry?"

"No," said Gayle. "Not in the least, even after four years with nothing to eat," laughed Gayle. "Maybe later we will be hungry."

Nancy and Carl continued on their way to the pilot's cabin on the third floor. They saw a few people on the third floor checking dials and computer screens in a room full of electronics equipment. Two men passed them, who were dressed in uniforms that had protective lead shields sown on the front of the uniforms.

"I suppose they are on their way to service the nuclear reactors and engines," said Carl.

"Looks that way," answered Nancy.

When they got to the pilot's cabin they knocked on the door and went in. Colonel Smith, Albert Haynes, and Charles Richardson were already on duty. Colonel Smith was looking at a map that was displayed on a large computer screen.

"Hello, Nancy and Carl," Colonel Smith greeted them with a smile on his face. "You look healthy and eager to get back to work."

"Hello, Colonel Smith," said Nancy. "Yes, we feel fine."

"The crew is checking all the spaceship's systems. Everything is in good order," said Colonel Smith.

"Albert Haynes and Charles Richardson appear to be very busy over there at the table by the ship's computer," said Nancy.

"Yes," said Colonel Smith. "They are investigating our options for approaching Titan. They are using that fan envelope that we talked about soon after we left the Dynasty base."

"Now that we are up close to Saturn," asked Carl, "is it obvious that having Saturn to our back, when we approach Titan, will make it difficult for the Philadelphians on Titan to see us?"

"Well, the gases of Saturn give the planet a roiling appearance," said Colonel Smith. "Also, the Philadelphians will have to look toward Saturn to see us, and that will tend to overload their detection equipment. It is something like keeping the sun behind you when you plan an air attack on earth. It is difficult for the defender to look into the sun while trying to aim his guns at an approaching airplane."

"How long will it take, do you think, for Albert and Charles to decide on the optimal approach?" asked Nancy.

"Maybe just today or tomorrow," answered Colonel Smith.

"Is there any sign yet of a Philadelphian reconnaissance space craft?" asked Carl.

"Not yet," answered Colonel Smith. "We turned our radars on for a while this morning and made some search scans. Nothing showed up."

"Right now the reconnaissance spaceships have to spot us on their own," said Carl. "But once we get around Saturn, the radars at the Philadelphian base on Titan might be able to spot us."

"Yes, but we will have Saturn behind us then and that will give their radars some trouble," said Colonel Smith.

Nancy asked, "Do you suppose, Colonel Smith, that the giant armada that we left Titan with years ago returned to Titan after their encounter with the Dynasty?"

"I imagine some of them did," answered Colonel Smith. "The cargo ship we were on was captured and some Philadelphian ships were destroyed. But, I suppose quite a few of the ships in that Philadelphian fleet got back here."

"So, no doubt the Philadelphians, today, are watching for any Dynasty spaceships which might have followed them back," said Carl.

"No doubt," said Colonel Smith.

Albert Haynes and Charles Richardson walked up and Albert said with a smile, "It is nice to see you, Nancy and Carl. How do you feel after the long sleep?"

"Just fine, Albert," said Nancy. "How are you?"

"I am fine," said Albert.

"Hi, Charles," said Nancy.

"Hello, Nancy and Carl," said Charles Richardson. "You both look healthy and energetic."

Nancy and Carl laughed. "We noticed a few people on the way up here. The crew seems to be checking out the ship's equipment."

"Yes, everyone has his assigned duty," said Colonel Smith.

"Colonel Smith," said Albert Haynes, "we have come up with what we think might be the optimal approach to Titan."

"Fine," said Colonel Smith. "Can you put it up on the computer screen?"

Albert Haynes touched a few knobs on the console and three simulations of our spaceship's flight path came up on the screen. They were three different views of the same fight path. Charles pressed a knob and a light spot representing our ship started moving on each of the three simulated paths.

"You can see," said Albert Haynes, "that we keep Saturn behind us as much as possible, as we approach Titan."

"Yes, it looks good," said Colonel Smith.

"If you look carefully at the paths," said Charles Richardson, "you can see the numbers 1 through 10. The numbers represent the days in the approach. Number 1 is where we are now."

"OK," said Colonel Smith, "it looks fine. As soon as we have a favorable report on all the ship's systems, we will embark on our plan."

"Everything is proceeding smoothly here," said Carl. "Maybe, Nancy and I will go back to the recreation room and see if everybody came out of their sleep OK."

Nancy said, "Maybe I can work up an appetite pretty soon."

When Nancy and Carl passed through the mess hall only two people were seated at a table, trying to eat. Carl and Nancy passed on to the recreation room.

"Here is where everybody is," exclaimed Nancy.

"Looks like nearly a hundred people are here," said Carl.

"There are George and Carol," said Nancy. Nancy and Carl headed in that direction.

"Hi, George and Carol," said Nancy.

"Hello, Nancy and Carl," returned Carol.

Nancy and Carl sat down on the couch opposite them.

"So, what have you heard from the decision makers?" asked George.

"The approach path has been chosen," said Carl. "And we are about to embark on it."

"We've all heard that we are going to approach Titan from the direction of Saturn," said Carol. "But, when will that be?"

"Ten days from now," answered Nancy. "That is, if the spaceship is in good condition, we will start on day one right now."

"Is there any indication of anything wrong?" asked Carol.

"No," answered Carl.

"I am a pessimist," said George. "I think we will be attacked by the Philadelphians on the way in."

"Oh, stop it, George," said Carol.

"You might be right," said Carl. "All we've got to defend ourselves with is one rocket launcher, plus a bunch of rockets."

"That's all they could find in the junk yard at the Dynasty base," said Nancy.

"Albert Haynes said they found a lot of radar jamming equipment and put that on board," said Carl.

"Well, that will help," said George.

"Out of the 100 or so passengers, we ought to have some veteran trained in the use of rockets," said Carl.

"Yes, Colonel Smith has already inducted them into service," said George.

"We won't be on the same side of Saturn as Titan for several days," put in Nancy. "So, they won't see us and we won't have to worry until then."

"Have you people seen the mess hall menu yet?" asked Carol.

"No. Have you?" asked Nancy.

"Yes," answered Carol. She took the menu out of her bag and began studying it. "The menu lists baked ham, escalloped potatoes, and green beans. When was that made do you think?"

"At least four years ago," answered Nancy with a smile, "and then frozen."

"How about apple tort and vanilla ice cream for desert," continued Carol.

"Magic," exclaimed Carl.

# Chapter 12

Three days later Nancy and Carl entered the mess hall at 7:30 am. They sat next to George and Carol.

"Did you look out the window this morning and see Titan?" asked Carol

"No," answered Nancy. "Is it there?"

"Yes," said George. "You can just see it coming around the side of Saturn."

"That means we will soon be in their field of vision," said Carl, "and they might see us."

"We are fortunate that they haven't been scouting or reconnoitering on the far side of Saturn all this time," said George. "They might have seen us when we first slowed down from nine tenths the speed of light."

"Maybe Colonel Smith will reduce our distance from Saturn pretty soon," said Nancy. "That should make it more difficult for the Philadelphians to see us."

"We could go up to the pilot's cabin after breakfast, Nancy, and check if we have entered on our approach path to Titan," said Carl.

"OK," said Nancy.

"These eggs and bacon actually taste right," said Carol, "in spite of the fact that they were frozen four years ago."

"Yes," said Nancy. "The cereal tastes the way it should, also."

"While you're up there in the pilot's cabin," said George, "ask Colonel Smith what our plan of action is supposed to be when we touch down on Titan."

"I will," said Carl.

They left the mess hall after having a cup of coffee.

"It looks like nearly everybody is in the mess hall," said Nancy as they made their way toward the pilot's cabin.

"Yes. They look happy and confidant," said Carl.

When they entered the pilot's cabin, Albert Haynes and Charles Richardson greeted them with, "Hello Nancy and Carl. How are you today?"

"Hi, Albert and Charles," responded Nancy. "Do you two and Colonel Smith have your cabins near the pilot's cabin? You people are on duty here quite a bit."

"Yes. Colonel Smith and Albert and I all have our separate cabins down the hall a short distance," said Charles Richardson.

"We have worked out a schedule," said Albert Haynes, "whereby one of us is on duty here in the pilot's cabin during the night. All three of us are here during the day."

"We can see Titan now. So, I suppose they can see us if they look this way," said Carl.

"Our spaceship is a lot smaller than the moon Titan," said Charles Richardson. "So, they have to be looking carefully for us in order to see us."

"Have you detected any radar scans coming our way?" asked Nancy.

"Nor yet," answered Charles Richardson.

"Have we embarked yet on our approach trajectory?" asked Carl.

"We just started on it this morning," answered Colonel Smith. "Our flight plan is just about in the middle of that fan shaped envelope of advantageous flight paths we worked out when we were back at the Dynasty base."

"Our altitude above Saturn is being reduced right now," said Albert Haynes. "We will approach Titan from below."

"We turn our radar on periodically to search for Philadelphian spaceships," said Colonel Smith. "We leave it off most of the time so they can't detect our radar scans."

"Have you seen a Philadelphian spaceship on the radar, yet?" asked Nancy.

"Once so far," answered Albert Haynes. "But it was a long distance away and was not coming in our direction."

"There is one on our radar screen now," shouted Colonel Smith, excitedly.

"It is at 10 o'clock and approaching. Two hours out. Sound the general alarm."

At that moment, a loud siren was heard throughout the spaceship.

All passengers had been told what to do in drills the first day and by instruction notices posted inside all cabins. The people who had been assigned to the rocket launcher ran to their station. Those assigned to the radar jamming equipment ran to their duty stations. The people manning the engines and controls in the pilot cabin were at their stations. Everyone else went to his cabin.

"He is asking us to identify ourselves," said Colonel Smith.

"He is not close enough yet to notice that we have the shape of a Dynasty ship," said Carl.

"Every thing in the junk yard we used to build this ship has the Dynasty shape," said Albert Haynes.

"Maybe we can elude him by changing course," said Colonel Smith, "and then jam his radars with our equipment."

Accordingly, he rapidly changed course.

Colonel Smith spoke into his microphone, "Radar room, can you get a fix on his position?"

"Not yet, Sir," came back the answer from the operator of the jamming equipment.

"Radio room reporting sir," came from the pilot cabin speaker. "We just heard a message from that reconnaissance spaceship to Titan headquarters. They think we are a Dynasty spaceship."

"The Philadelphians will have a whole fleet of spaceships up here in a day or two," said Carl.

"I am going to change our course periodically and jam his radars," said Colonel Smith. "Maybe, we can elude him."

"What can we do with our rocket launcher?" asked Nancy.

"Our rocket launcher is too small to seriously damage one of those spaceships," said Albert Haynes. "There is a radar antenna pod sticking out from the port side of those spaceships. We might be able to hit that pod with our rockets and disable their radar."

"But we have to be pretty close to that spaceship to take an accurate aim at the pod," said Carl.

"Radar room, sir," came over the pilot cabin speaker.

"Go ahead, radar room," said Colonel Smith.

"The Philadelphian spaceship passed us by and is now turning around and is coming toward us," came over the pilot cabin speaker.

"Radar room. How far back are they?" asked Colonel Smith.

"Radar Room. They are a long way back, sir. It might take them an hour to catch up."

"I think we will turn off our radar and continue our zigzag path," said Colonel Smith. "We may lose them."

"Radar room," said Colonel Smith into his microphone.

"Radar room, sir," came over the loud speaker.

"Radar room. Turn off your radar at this time," said Colonel Smith.

"Radar room. Yes, sir," came the answer over the speaker.

After an hour, Colonel Smith desisted from ordering a zigzag path and resumed our path to Titan.

"Tomorrow, we will probably encounter a squadron of Philadelphians looking for us," said Colonel Smith.

"Yes, but we are flying low to Saturn and they will be flying high," said Charles Richardson. "They might not see us."

Nancy and Carl were in the pilot's cabin early the next day.

"Radar room," came over the pilot cabin speaker at 9 am.

"Go ahead, radar room," answered Colonel Smith.

"Radar room. A flight of Philadelphian spaceships are passing high overhead," came over the speaker.

"Good. They don't see us," said Nancy.

"Radar room," came over the speaker at 11am.

"Radar room, sir. There is a Philadelphian spaceship coming up behind us. It is about an hour out. Maybe it's the ship we eluded yesterday," came over the pilot cabin speaker.

"Rocket launcher room," said Colonel Smith into his microphone.

"Rocket launcher room, sir," was the answer over the speaker.

"Rocket Launcher room," said Colonel Smith into his microphone, "a Philadelphian spaceship will approach us from the rear in about an hour. It has a radar antenna pod on its port side. Launch several rockets at that pod when the spaceship comes into range."

"Rocket Launcher room. Yes sir," was the answer over the pilot cabin speaker.

An hour later, the radio room announced over the pilot cabin speaker, "Radio room, sir."

"Go ahead, radio room," answered Colonel Smith.

"Radio room. The Philadelphian spaceship approaching from the rear, demands that we stop and prepare for their boarding party."

"Radio room. I got your message," returned Colonel Smith into his microphone.

"Rocket Launch room," said Colonel Smith into his microphone.

"Rocket Launch room, sir," came over the speaker.

"Rocket Launch room," said Colonel Smith, "can you get a proper aim on their radar pod?"

"Rocket Launcher room. Yes sir, we have a proper aim and will fire two rockets in a few seconds," came over the loud speaker;

At that moment, Nancy and Carl saw two rockets leave their spaceship and strike the radar pods of the Philadelphian ship.

Colonel Smith saw it also, and said over his microphone, "Engine room, full ahead."

The Philadelphian ship could not follow our swerving path very well without radar and soon fell far behind.

"They have probably radioed ahead to Titan saying that a Dynasty ship is on the way," said Colonel Smith.

"So, do you think our advantage of coming in from the Saturn direction has been lost?" asked Nancy.

"Well, they'll be looking for us to come in from the direction of Saturn," said Carl. "If it hadn't been for this attack, they might not look this way."

"That's true," said Colonel Smith, "but we still have the advantage derived from the mottled background provided by Saturn. They'll have some difficulty separating us from the Saturn background."

"Also, if they don't shoot us down, they will be looking for Dynasty people on the ground, not earth people," said Nancy. "I don't know if that will help us in any way."

"Titan will be looking for Dynasty soldiers," said Albert Haynes. "That ought to give them a certain mind set."

"There are going to be about a hundred of us looking for empty rooms and partially empty factory space in a few days," said Charles Richardson.

"It would have been a lot better if we could have entered their domain unseen and unexpected," said Nancy.

"Our immediate concern is to land there without being attacked and destroyed," said Colonel Smith.

"Yes, we can worry about our accommodations and living conditions later," said Carl.

"We can't just land outside the base and walk in unnoticed," said Colonel Smith. "Remember the temperature is that of liquid nitrogen."

"The base must be like something floating on liquid nitrogen," said Charles Richardson.

"We will hover around one of their space ports and wait for the port to open to let one of their spaceships in or out," said Colonel Smith. "Then we will enter the same time their space ship passes through the portal."

"Our survival, then, depends on whether we can hover about a portal and not be seen," said Nancy.

"That might not be as hard as it sounds," said Albert Haynes. "The base has a highly irregular shape with lots of projections on its outer surface."

"So, we approach the base under its radar cone and at night when most of their inhabitants are asleep," said Nancy.

"Yes, we have to stay under its radar cone, swept out by its antennas, to avoid being seen by their radar," said Carl.

"Actually, our spaceship has the stealth design characteristics; that is, it has both the shape and the materials of a stealth ship," said Colonel Smith.

"Therefore, they should have a hard time seeing us on radar," said Nancy.

"That's right," said Colonel Smith.

"By tomorrow night we should be up near a Titan portal," said Charles Richardson, "where we can loiter and wait for our chance to enter the base."

"Carl, let's go back to the recreation room and tell the others what the plan is," said Nancy.

"OK," answered Carl.

They left the pilot cabin and passed through the areas that held the radar equipment, transmitters, receivers, and other electronic equipment. On their way down the stairway to the first floor they tried to figure out how a base could exist on a moon with liquid nitrogen all around. To be floating on liquid nitrogen seemed too bizarre to comprehend. When they passed through the mess hall, they noticed only a few people sitting around sipping a drink or eating a snack.

Nancy looked at her watch and said, "It is almost three more hours to dinner."

Carl asked, "Are you finally starting to get your appetite back?"

"Yes," answered Nancy. "The food is surprisingly good, even if it has been frozen for four years."

"They entered the recreation room and as usual almost everybody was there. They noticed George and Carol and headed toward them.

"Hi, Nancy and Carl," called Carol as they approached.

"Hello, Carol," returned Carl.

"Have you two been up in the pilot cabin finding out the latest developments?" asked George.

"Yes," answered Nancy. "We thought we would come back and describe the current plan."

Carl and Nancy told George and Carol, and any others who came over to listen, what the current plan was.

"So, tomorrow night will be a crucial time for us," said Janet.

"Of course, we might have to loiter around the space portal for days before a Philadelphian spaceship goes in or out," said Gayle.

"Yes, that is true," said Carl.

"Well, let's hope the Philadelphians don't detect us and put us in prison for another year," put in Gayle.

"We have fuel enough to stay here for a very long time, I imagine," said George. "But we have a very limited supply of food for everybody to eat."

"Is morale pretty good among all the people?" asked Nancy.

"Oh, yes," said Janet.

"Everybody cheered when our rocket hit the radar antenna of that Philadelphian cruiser, yesterday," said Gayle.

"That Philadelphian spaceship must have sent a radio message to Titan describing the encounter," said George. "Could they tell up there in the pilot's cabin if any Philadelphian spaceships have left Titan to come our way?"

"I don't think we are running our radar constantly to check if anything is coming our way," said Carl.

"We don't want' to emit radar energy all the time," said Nancy. "If we did, they could probably detect us."

"Tomorrow night everybody will be tense as we approach the Titan portal," said Janet, "but tonight we are a little more relaxed. Does anyone know what is on the menu in the mess hall tonight?"

"Baked ham and escalloped potatoes," said Nancy. "I read the menu as we passed through the mess hall."

With that everybody returned to their afternoon past time. Quite a few people were engaged in card games or chess. Others were reading books they had found on book shelves in the recreation room. Carl and Nancy went for a walk through the halls until it was meal time in the mess hall.

The next morning when Nancy and Carl went to the pilot cabin, they noticed that Titan was becoming very prominent before them as they looked out the window.

"If we were to look out a rear window now, would Saturn still fill most of the view?" Nancy asked.

"Yes, it would," said Albert Haynes. "In fact I can switch this computer screen to show the rear view."

As he entered the command, a view of Saturn appeared on the screen.

Carl pointed forward out the window. "Have you located the Philadelphian base yet in this view of Titan?"

"Yes, we have," said Colonel Smith. "It is directly ahead of us. We should be there by about 8 pm tonight."

"With our radar off and all other electronic emission off will we be able to see it fairly well at 8pm?" asked Nancy.

"Oh, yes," said Charles Richardson. "By midnight we will be right next to the base. We will try to find some protruding structure to hide behind."

"Our stealth qualities must be very effective," said Carl, "because they haven't noticed us yet."

"Yes, that is true," said Colonel Smith.

"Things are going to be very tense up here around 8 pm tonight," Nancy said to Carl.

"You are absolutely right," replied Carl.

"Well let's go to the mess hall and have breakfast," Nancy said. "We only have a few hours of comparative calm."

"OK," answered Carl.

After breakfast they made their way to the recreation room and talked to the others.

"The stress is growing around here," said George. "Just imagine, we might have to hide around here for days before a Philadelphian ship goes in or out."

"Once we get inside," said Janet, "and we must be confident about this—we will get inside—we must land someplace and quickly find lodgings for ourselves."

"We have been drawing maps of this base from memory," said Gayle.

"It is quite huge." said Janet. "It is about three quarters of a mile long and nearly a half mile wide."

"There are hundreds of buildings for us to live in," said Gayle.

"We have a little over a hundred people," said Carol. "We will probably be living in five or six different buildings."

"We will have to establish a communications system," said Gayle. "Then we can hold meetings."

"It might take a whole year for all of us to get back to earth," said Janet. "Only a few might be able to stow away aboard each shuttle to earth."

This happy conversation occupied much of the afternoon.

"Right now," said Nancy, "I'm hungry. What's for supper tonight?"

"Roast turkey, sweet potatoes, and cranberries," said someone in the crowd.

"Excellent," said Carl. "I haven't had that in a long time."

With that, Nancy and Carl departed for the mess hall.

"This mess hall reminds me of the Navy," said Carl. "You walk down the cafeteria line with a compartmentalized tray. If you hold your tray out near an item, they slap some food on it. If you don't want an item, you hold your tray back."

"The turkey looks and smells good," said Nancy.

A short time later, Janet and Gayle came in and sat at the next table over from Nancy and Carl.

"They have two kinds of ice cream for desert," said Gayle, "and two kinds of topping."

"What are the toppings?" asked Carl.

"Chocolate and something else," answered Gayle.

After supper Carl and Nancy went to the pilot's cabin.

Upon entering the pilot cabin Nancy gripped Carl's arm. Titan completely filled the window.

"Hi, Carl and Nancy," said Albert Haynes. "You can clearly see the Philadelphian base now."

"The space port is that structure over there on the left," said Colonel Smith. "It looks like a dome with a long horizontal door beneath it. The dome above the middle of the door is probably where the gate keeper sits."

"Apparently the door can ride on tracks," said Albert Haynes. "Part of it opens to the left and the other part opens to the right."

"Do you see that large structure to the right that projects outwards from the base?" asked Colonel Smith.

"Yes," said Carl.

"It doesn't seem to have any windows in it," continued Colonel Smith.

"I think you are right," said Carl. "Its walls are perfectly smooth."

"I think we can hide behind it and watch the space portal from there," said Colonel Smith.

"Yes, it would provide a good vantage point," said Nancy.

"It will be dark soon," continued Colonel Smith. "We will make our move when it's dark."

Colonel Smith and Charles Richardson turned their attention to the ship's controls.

"It is positively amazing that they haven't seen us," Nancy said to Carl.

"Our stealth qualities must be very effective," said Carl, "or Saturn behind us interferes very greatly with their detection equipment."

"How many Philadelphians do you think are on this base?" asked Nancy. "It must be about half a square mile in area."

"I don't know," said Carl. "It must be at least five thousand. That armada we traveled with to the Dynasty base on New Barstow must have had several thousand Philadelphian military people in it."

"It is getting dark quickly isn't it?" asked Nancy. "The light is pretty faint anyway. We are so far from the sun."

"Titan doesn't have a thick atmosphere of air and water like earth to bend the light rays around the planet. So, there is no long twilight," said Carl.

"So, it goes from light to dark fast," said Nancy.

Colonel Smith took his position in the pilot seat and grasped the steering wheel and accelerator. "All right, here we go," he said.

We slowly approached the long structure that projected out from the base. It had a few lights on it to demarcate its extremities but no other lights or windows. Colonel Smith positioned our ship just around the corner of the projection.

"I don't think anyone can see us here," said Colonel Smith. "Yet, our nose is sticking out enough so that we can see all the activity in the vicinity of the space portal.

"We are also out of the line of sight of anyone approaching the base," said Albert Haynes. "That is good for remaining concealed."

"How are we going to be ready to fly in when someone else flies in if we can't see then approaching?" asked Carl.

"We will have to watch the portal doors closely," said Charles Richardson. "When they slide open, we know someone is approaching or leaving."

"How do you plan to enter the portal door, Colonel Smith?" asked Nancy. "Is the door tall enough for us to fly underneath other spaceship?"

"We used our telescope earlier when it was still light," answered Colonel Smith, "and we figure the door is about 300 feet tall."

"Our space ship is 40 feet tall," said Albert Haynes.

"That would make a tight squeeze," responded Colonel Smith, "especially if the other ship is trying to go down the middle."

"I remember watching a World War II movie where a submarine entered a harbor that had under water gates by traveling underneath a ship entering the harbor," said Carl.

"Sometimes those submarines travel right behind service ships," put in Charles Richardson.

"We will fly under the spaceship up to the door," said Colonel Smith. "If he flies too low, we'll travel behind him."

"The main thing is to get through the gate." said Albert Haynes. "We can always land the spaceship fast and run for some building if we are seen."

"Yes, we have to get into the base," said Carl. "We can't live in this inhospitable environment."

"Even if we do get into the base undetected," said Nancy, "where would we conceal this big old spaceship?"

"Sooner or later, they are going to know we are here," said Carl.

"Right," said Nancy. "Our job will be to get aboard a shuttle to earth while they are searching for us in the wrong building."

"Yes. We will play cat and mouse," said Albert Haynes.

"Carl, let's go back to the recreation room and tell the others about the game plan," said Nancy.

"All right," said Carl.

As they walked back down the halls, Carl said, "I sure hope we can avoid capture. I would hate to be hauled off to another planet again."

"Think of the number of years spent on one of those trips," said Nancy. "That round trip to the Dynasty base took eight years."

When they entered the recreation room, many of the people were looking out the windows at the Titan base.

Carl and Nancy went up to Janet and Gayle. "Quite a sight isn't it?" asked Carl.

"Oh, Hi Carl and Nancy," said Gayle.

"Not a window in the whole wall," exclaimed Janet.

"Colonel Smith chose this place to hide," said Nancy.

"We are parked in a place where they can't see us," said Carl. "However, the nose of our spaceship juts out just far enough beyond the wall so that we have a good view of their space portal."

Many of the others had gathered around now to listen. They knew Nancy and Carl frequented the pilot cabin.

Nancy said, "Colonel Smith is going to fly us into the base by flying us either under or just behind some Philadelphian spaceship that is entering or leaving the base."

Carl continued, "The space portal consists of two big sliding doors, each one about 300 feet high and maybe 400 feet long."

Someone asked, "Isn't there a door someplace where we could just walk through? Park our ship outside and walk in."

"We would probably freeze to death trying," answered George.

"The Titan moon," he continued, "has a lot of liquid nitrogen about."

"Liquid nitrogen is below—200 degrees Fahrenheit," put in somebody.

"We have to fly in the portal door," said Nancy.

"They might see us doing it," said Carol, "but we don't have a choice."

"So, once we get in and land, we make a dash for the buildings," said George. "Is that it?"

"Pretty much," answered Carl.

"As I recall," said Janet, "there are a lot of buildings on the base. We should be able to find a few open doors."

"The whole base is covered over or has a curved ceiling as I recall," said Janet, "to protect against the cold I suppose."

"You can move about on the streets with just ordinary clothes on," said Nancy.

"We have a lot of people to conceal," said Carol. "There are about a hundred of us."

"We'll probably occupy several buildings," said Carl, "and work out an electronic system for use in communication."

"Last time we were here," said Carl, "Nancy and I got our clothes from discard stations and went grocery shopping in the garbage cans."

"We had an electric stove in our little room or den to use to cook the food," said Nancy.

Someone in the crowd said, "No doubt the big project will be to study the shuttle schedule to earth and find ways to smuggle people aboard from our communities."

"It will probably take lots of flights spread out over a year," said Carol.

"That's correct. Our immediate concern, however, is to pass through that space portal without being seen," said George.

"Well, I think that I will leave these worries for tomorrow and go to bed now. I am very tired," said Nancy.

The next morning when Nancy and Carl entered the pilot cabin Colonel Smith, Albert, and Charles were conferring at the central table.

"Hi, Nancy and Carl," said Charles Richardson.

"Hello," answered Nancy.

"We have been monitoring the Philadelphian traffic for the last 8 hours," said Colonel Smith. "During that time, two Philadelphian military spaceships went out and two others came in. Also, one shuttle ship to earth departed."

"When they rolled the portal doors open," said Nancy, "was there anyway you could tell whether a ship was entering or leaving? Or, did you just have to wait until the ship appeared?"

"Actually, we can tell," said Charles Richardson. "When a ship is arriving, those lights come on above the door to signal the pilot I suppose. But, when a ship leaves the lights don't come on."

"So, if we want to enter under some arriving ship, we watch for the lights," said Nancy.

"Right," responded Charles.

"When those two ships arrived recently, Colonel Smith, did there seem to be much room beneath them?" asked Carl.

"Unfortunately, they flew pretty low," answered Colonel Smith.

"They were both military ships, though," interjected Albert Haynes. "Maybe when the shuttle returns, it will fly a little higher."

"That would certainly make life easier for us," said Colonel Smith.

Just at that moment they saw the portal doors roll open.

"The lights are on," said Charles Richardson.

A minute later, a space shuttle from earth passed before them and entered the portal doors.

"They flew in high," said Colonel Smith in a jubilant voice. "That would give us plenty of room."

"How long would it take us to accelerate over there if we saw a space shuttle approaching?" asked Carl.

"It's only a thousand yards from here to the door," answered Colonel Smith. "I could easily accelerate over there in time."

"So, our entrance to the base could occur almost any day now," said Nancy.

Two days later, Nancy and Carl were in the pilot cabin early in the morning talking to Charles Richardson about establishing a communications system between the possibly ten or more separate groups of Californians that would form soon after the spaceship got inside the Titan base.

"Doors are opening," called out Albert Haynes. "The lights are on so it is an incoming ship."

Colonel Smith immediately took the pilot's seat and started our spaceship moving forward slowly. The incoming spaceship was not yet visible.

"There it is," called out Albert Haynes.

"It is a shuttle," said Colonel Smith.

He started moving the accelerator forward and steering around the projection behind which we were concealed.

"It is very large, isn't it?" asked Nancy.

"Yes, it is gigantic compared to us," answered Carl.

"We are right under it now," said Nancy. "You can look forward and backward, right and left, and it extends beyond us."

"Here we are at the portal door," said Carl.

"It looks like the shuttle is high enough," said Albert Haynes. "We should fit under it easily."

They passed though the door and proceeded down a long channel.

"I suppose if anybody looked at us passing by, we must look strange," said Charles Richardson. "They would see one big ship above and a little one underneath, passing down the channel."

The channel extended far down the length of the Titan space center. To either side could be seen a great many buildings.

"The buildings all seem grey in color and about two stories high," said Nancy.

"Yes, that semitransparent dome over the entire base is extraordinary," said Carl.

"It must be made of some extremely strong and durable plastic," said Albert Haynes.

"There are a few lights in each building, but over to the right there seems to be a lot of lights," said Nancy.

"Maybe that is where the Philadelphians live," remarked Charles Richardson.

"Do you think we are headed towards some sort of spaceship landing strip or warehouse region?" asked Albert.

"No doubt," answered Carl.

After a moment they came to a vast area of warehouses and parked spaceships.

"Look around," said Colonel Smith, "and see if you can spot a service and repair yard for spaceships."

"Yes, we could park there and not be noticed for several days," remarked Carl.

"That place to the far right looks like a service area," said Albert Haynes. "A number of spaceships are there and some of them have part of their fuselage opened up."

"I see it," said Colonel Smith.

# Chapter 13

It was early enough in the morning for it to still be fairly dark outside. There were lights on along the street but there weren't many people out yet.

"Carl and Nancy," said Colonel Smith, "please go back to the cabins and make sure everybody is up and dressed and ready to move."

Carl answered, "Yes, sir."

Nancy and Carl hurried to the second floor.

"I'll knock on doors on this side, you take the other side," said Carl.

A few people were looking out of their cabins with bewildered looks on their faces.

George opened his cabin door and Carl said, "We are inside the base. Get dressed and be ready to move." Carl then passed to the next door.

A half an hour later, nearly everybody was in the recreation room in a state of excitement and apprehension.

Carl announced, "We will be landing soon and will have to run to find buildings to live in. Colonel Smith will notify us over the loud speaker system."

"If you have any belongings you want to take with you, you had better get them now and keep then near you," said Nancy.

Carl and Nancy went back to the pilot cabin. Upon entering, Charles Richardson said, "The shuttle ship is moving towards a large landing field up ahead."

As they approached the landing field they noticed a lot of other spaceships parked on the ground. At one end of the field some of the spaceships looked as if they were being repaired or dismantled.

"That repair field over there looks like a good place to land our spaceship," said Colonel Smith.

"Yes, they might not find this ship for days," said Albert Haynes.

"That should give everybody a chance to find a concealed living space," said Nancy.

Colonel Smith flew the spaceship over to the repair region and, after looking around for Philadelphians, landed the ship quietly.

Colonel Smith picked up the microphone and said, "Good morning everyone, we have landed inside the Philadelphian base. We are in what appears to be a spaceship repair region. No Philadelphians are in sight at this time. There are quite a few buildings within a half mile of here in almost every direction. Form small groups of eight or ten and prepare to set out in search of lodgings. We will take a careful look around the area and then open the doors in about 15 minutes."

Nancy and Carl hurried back to their cabin.

"I don't have many personal belongings to take," said Nancy.

"Me either," said Carl.

They left and headed for the exit door. Everybody was standing at the exit door, speaking in excited tones, and forming small groups.

Carl and Nancy found George, Carol, Janet, and Gayle. "We might as well form a group," said Nancy.

"Yes, let's." said Janet and Gayle together. "The six of us will make a good group," put in George.

Colonel Smith's voice came over the speaker system. "No Philadelphians are in sight. We will now turn off all of our lights and open the door. Please speak quietly. We should be able to meet each other in the next few days and establish a communication system."

With that, the lights went out and the door opened.

They stepped out onto the ground and started moving away from their spaceship.

"Which building should we head for?" asked Nancy.

Let's get away from the landing field and move toward the region where most of the people live," suggested Carol.

"OK," said Carl. "Do you see that street over there with all the colored lights. I think that is the shopping area."

"Let's head that way," said Gayle.

As they approached the area, they noticed a large building that had few lights in it.

"That might be a storage building or warehouse," said George. "We might be able to find living space in there."

They approached the building and started trying the doors.

"This door is open," said Carol.

They all looked in. There was a large space on the ground floor with boxes stacked around. Several stair cases led upward.

"Looks good to me," said Carl. "Let's investigate some of those upper floors."

After about twenty minutes they found a large storage room with a lot of cartons stacked in several aisles.

"This looks promising," said George. He climbed to the top of the stacks and started moving cartons around. After a few minutes, George looked over the edge of the stacks and called down, "We can push the cartons about and make living spaces."

Carl came over and said, "I just found a sink; it is attached to the building's water pipe system. We can easily fashion a bathroom out of it."

"Let's stay here," said Carol.

They all started climbing the cartons and selecting living spaces. They found some pipes lying on the floor and spent the next couple of hours making a bathroom and a cooking area over by the pipes and sink that Carl had found.

"Maybe we can find some cloth or padding in some of these cartons and furnish our little living spaces with beds and chairs," said Nancy.

By the time it was light outside the six of them had made their living cubicles tolerable. The cubicles were on top of the stacked cartons and not likely to be seen by any of the workers in the building.

"Our next step is to go shopping in the alleys," said Nancy. "We can find suitable clothing in the discard bins."

"The restaurants throw a lot of edible food into the garbage cans behind their restaurants," said Carl.

"Sometimes they throw away frozen packages of food," put in Nancy. "That is certainly edible if you find it before it thaws."

They climbed down to the first floor and passed out into the alley.

"We better avoid the main streets," said Carol, "until we have their style of clothes to wear."

After rummaging around in two alleys for an hour, they retuned to their building.

"I found a nice red sweater," said Carol.

"I found a pretty skirt," said Janet. "I hope the shoes I found fit."

"Well, I found a brown pants and a shirt," said George. "It looks like it was made on earth."

"Yes, they don't just get military hardware from down there," said Carl. "I got a pair of jeans."

"We better find a junk yard next," said Nancy. "We need to get an electric hot plate on which to cook."

"Yes, you're right," said Carol.

"This place is pretty small," said George. "It can't be too far to a junk yard."

They divided into two groups and set out in search of a junk yard. It wasn't long before Nancy, Carl, and Janet came upon one. Carl boosted the girls over the fence and then climbed over himself. They found a lot of the typical discards of homes supplied by the American electronics industry. They called George and the other girls over.

"Wow," said Janet, "they must bring everything marketed by the American retail industry up here on those shuttles."

"We could take one of those small refrigerators over there," said Gayle, pointing at a pile of kitchen appliances.

"Also, one of those electric hot plates to cook on," said Nancy.

"There is an electronic entertainment center over there," said Gayle. "They have CD players and TV's."

"I suppose they produce electric power with nuclear reactors," said Carl. "That would supply the entire base."

"The TV's are connected by cable, no doubt," said George. "I wonder where their studio is and what the programs could be."

"Can you imagine the kind of music these people listen to?" asked Carol.

"Probably ROCK," answered Gayle. "Everybody else does."

"OK, let's just grab what we can carry this time," said Carl. "We have to get it over the fence and down the alley without being seen."

They just took a refrigerator, a hot plate, a couple of lamps, and some extension cords. When they got back they strung the extension cords and tried out the refrigerator and hot plate.

"Wonderful," exclaimed Carol. "Everything works."

"I am glad of that. I was afraid we might have to make a second trip to the junk yard if they didn't work," said George.

"Well it's time for grocery shopping now," said Nancy. "Let's hit the alleys again."

"We better walk over to the main shopping area and look for restaurants," said Carl.

"Then we can go into the allies behind the restaurants to find garbage cans."

They set out for the streets where a lot of Philadelphians were walking about.

"Talk very softly," said Nancy. "We don't want them to overhear our language."

When they entered the main concourse, they discovered many shops.

"There must be hundreds of Philadelphians shopping or just walking about," exclaimed Janet.

"Don't the people around here work?" asked Gayle. "It's the middle of the day."

"There are two restaurants up ahead on our side of the street," said Carl. "Let's just pass by and see what they are serving."

They passed by the first restaurant and noticed about twenty tables. About half were occupied.

"Smells like beef steak and onions to me," said Nancy.

"I think you're right," answered Carl.

"So they shuttle raw beef up here," said George.

"Certainly smells like it," said Carol.

Turning around and counting, Carl said, "This is the fifteenth establishment from the corner. We can count that off when we are in the alley."

"Let's hope some of the beef comes frozen," said Nancy. "Unfrozen raw beef isn't going to be much good in the garbage cans."

They passed on to the second restaurant.

"Is that Chinese food?" asked Janet.

"Certainly looks like it from the pictures on the wall," said George.

"What kind of food do you think the Philadelphians ate on their own planer?" asked Gayle.

"Who knows," answered Janet.

"There's another restaurant on the other side of the street up ahead," said George.

They crossed the street.

"They don't have many automobiles here," said Gayle.

"They don't want to waste time and nuclear fuel hauling gasoline up here," responded Carl.

Nancy grabbed Carl's arm. "Look," she said, nodding toward a window, "that is what they watch on television."

They glanced through the window as they past by. Three Philadelphians were sitting at a table, facing the TV, and talking.

"Do you think it is a news broadcast or some kind of indoctrination program?" asked Carl.

"I don't know," said Nancy.

"We still have our Philadelphian to English dictionaries haven't we?" asked Carl.

"Yes, I kept them of course," answered Nancy.

"We will have to get one of those TV sets in the junk yard," said Nancy.

"Do you suppose they have entertainment shows at night on TV?" asked Gayle.

"We will find out in a few days," said George.

They passed on to a restaurant.

"This seems to be a more upscale restaurant," said Janet.

"Yes, notice the table cloths on the tables and the fancy table decorations," said Gayle.

"Also, the waiters have white coats on," added Nancy.

"Several of the patrons are wearing uniforms," said George.

"Yes. This is a kind of military base," said Carl. "So, the higher social strata will be military officers."

"The food has a more delicate aroma," said Nancy. "It is a little hard to identify."

"Maybe, it is their national dish from home," suggested Carol.

"There is a server with what appears to be roast duck or chicken," said Janet.

"The garbage cans in the alley behind here will probably have better food," said George.

They decided to walk on up the street to see what other shops were there. They found clothing shops and electronic shops.

"Look at that shop across the street," said George. "Is that a newspaper and book store?"

"Certainly looks like it," answered Carol.

"Do you think they have news stories about earth?" asked Gayle.

"They might," answered Carol.

"But how can we read their papers?" asked Gayle.

"Carl and I put together a Philadelphian to English dictionary when we were here before," said Nancy, "and I still have it."

"They probably cast their old papers in a trash can in the alley," said Carl. "We could look there."

"Let's just pass through one of the clothing stores," said Carol. "We don't have to say anything. We can just keep moving."

"OK," said Janet. "We won't say a word or touch anything."

They crossed the street again, and the four women went into the store. George and Carl remained outside.

"Do you think they have some kind of regular working hours here?" asked George. "There are so many people on the street."

"They must," answered Carl. "They make all those spaceships here."

"Maybe they have five or ten thousand people here," continued George.

"Could be," returned Carl.

"They must have a good engineering staff to design those things," said George.

"And a big assembly plant," added Carl. "I wonder which building is the spaceship factory."

"I don't know," said George. "But we shouldn't get too near it. They probably have pretty good security around it."

"For what reason would they need security?" asked Carl. "Do you suppose they worry about sabotage?"

"Who knows," answered George. "The people who run those places are always worrying about something."

"Here come the women," said Carl.

"They have got some of the top of the line names in there," said Carol.

"I wonder who is paying for all this," said George.

"The American tax payer is paying for it." said Carl.

"Right," said George. "The government buys this stuff from the stores on earth and then hands it over to the Philadelphians."

"It looked to me like the people in the store were using cards to pay for their purchases," said Nancy.

"The Philadelphian administration, or what ever you want to call it, has to operate their system in an orderly fashion," suggested Carl. "So, if you work so many hours in the factory, your card gets some buying power assigned to it."

"I doubt these people give anything of value to America for these commercial goods," said George.

"No. America can't bring any pressure to bear on them," added Carl.

"Do you suppose the Philadelphians give spaceship technology to America in exchange for consumable goods?" asked George.

"It's a thought," responded Carl. "But I don't think America is in a bargaining position. America is way behind these people, militarily."

"I think you're right," said Nancy. "The Philadelphians just dictate to America."

"Well, let's head to the alleys in search of food," said Carl.

"Should we try this fancy restaurant first?" asked Carol.

"Why not," answered George.

They went around the block and walked back through the alley to the approximate location of the restaurant.

"Is this the garbage can?" asked Carol.

"It is hard to tell," answered George. "The dumpsters all look the same and the back of the buildings look the same."

"We have counted down the right number," said Carl. "Let's just look in a few of these cans."

In the second dumpster they found the restaurant refuse. Nancy looked inside.

"Is there any frozen stuff?" asked Janet.

"Yes. I'll toss it to you," answered Nancy.

"I'll keep watch," said Gayle.

"Here comes some bags of rice and potatoes," said Nancy.

"There are a lot of cans of vegetables," said Nancy. "Here they come."

"Why do you suppose they toss all of this stuff out?" asked George.

"I don't know," answered Carl. "Maybe they got a new shipment on the last shuttle."

"Here are a bunch of boxes of cereal and flour," said Nancy. "Coming your way."

"Nobody's coming, yet," said George.

"Let's just grab all they've got that looks edible while we are at it," said Carl.

They had four bags of groceries when they stopped.

"That wasn't bad," said Janet, as they departed from the alley.

"Did you get any cooking oil and spices?" asked Gayle.

"I found cooking oil," answered Nancy, "but no spices."

"An odd thing about this place is that there are no seasons," said Carl. "It is either light or dark, but no change in the weather."

"There is no weather," said George. "The atmosphere is artificially generated."

"Yes. It is designed for efficient working conditions," put in Janet.

"You see that car coming down the road?" said Carl.

"Yes," answered Gayle.

"That may be their police department," said Carl.

"Lets step into one of these stores while it passes," said George.

An electric powered car with two uniformed occupants passed.

Nancy copied down on her bag what had been written on the side of the car. "I'll check out those words in our dictionary when we get home," she said.

They resumed their walk and got back to their building in a short time. Carol and Nancy cooked a pretty good meal of spaghetti and meat balls that night. They used the plates and eating utensils that Janet had the foresight to pick up at the junk yard earlier.

"Tomorrow we should go back to that junk yard and get some electronic gear," said George.

"Yes," said Carol. "We should definitely get one of those TV's now that we know they have broadcasts."

"We should also look for some kind of electronic communication equipment," said Carl. "We need to talk to the other groups."

"Is there some way to use old cell phones?" asked Janet.

"Well, we don't want them listening in on our conversations," said George.

"Albert Haynes is in one of the groups," put in Janet. "And he is an electrical engineer."

"Maybe he can develop a private radio signal for us," said Nancy.

"We have to contact those people in person first," said Carl.

"They probably go to the same shopping district we went to," said Nancy.

"I didn't notice them today," said Carol.

"Could there be another shopping district?" asked George.

"The one we went to is the only brightly lighted area," answered Carl.

"Maybe we should post a sort of guard there during the days to watch for them," said Janet.

"We could establish watch hours," said Gayle.

"I'll take the first two hours tomorrow morning," said Janet.

"I'll take the second two hours," said Gayle.

"Put me down for the third two," said Carol.

"OK. That's six hours tomorrow morning and afternoon," said Carl. "Let's see if we establish contact with that."

George got out two decks of cards that he had been carrying around. They played pinochle for a couple of hours.

The next day Janet stood her watch while the others went back to the junk yard. Carol and Nancy found a TV set and carried it back to their building. Gayle hunted for some music electronics.

George came over to Carl and said, "I found a couple of boxes of electronic parts and tools over here. Do you want to take a look?"

212 Donald Christopherson

They looked in the box and found an assortment of circuit boards, board connectors, and rolls of wire.

"All this stuff looks useful to me," said Carl. "Maybe Albert Haynes can use it."

"Over here are some tools," said George. They found soldering irons, solder, and boxes of connectors.

"I wonder why they throw all this good stuff away," said George.

"I can't imagine," said Carl.

"Do you suppose they got a new supply?" asked George.

"Or maybe some new circuit boards that make this stuff obsolete," said Carl.

"Anyway, let's take a bag of it back and ask Albert Haynes if it is useful," said George.

"OK," said Carl.

They put most of it in a bag and headed back to their building. The girls already had the TV working and Nancy was trying to translate the speech.

"It seems to be a kind of news broadcast," said Nancy.

"They talked about the development of one of their spaceships," said Carol. "They also talked about the

Barstonians and maybe about some other Philadelphians some place."

"We found a bunch of electronics stuff," said Carl, holding up their bag.

"I wonder if Janet made contact with any of the others," said George.

"It is just about my turn to go on watch," said Gayle. "I better get ready."

When Janet got back she said breathlessly, "I met four of the others. Not Albert Haynes but some of those we knew in the recreation room aboard our spaceship."

"Where are they staying?" asked Carl.

"Well we drew a kind of map of the whole complex and marked our buildings," said Janet.

"Yes. That is a good idea," said Carl. "We have to know where everybody lives."

"But we have to code which buildings we are in," said George. "That way, if the police find one of our maps they won't be able to figure out where we are."

"What we can do," said Carl, "is get one of their official maps—if there are any—and on a separate sheet of paper, list the buildings where everybody is staying."

"Yes," said Nancy, "that sounds like a good idea."

Nancy and Carol made lunch. They prepared fried ham and French fries.

"Ah," said George. "This has great flavor, even if it is not very good for the heart."

An hour later, Gayle returned from her watch. "I have good news," she said. "I found Albert Haynes and Charles Richardson. And they know where eight others are."

"Can you draw a map showing their buildings?" asked George.

"I already have," answered Gayle.

"We have to have a meeting tomorrow with Albert Haynes," said Carl. "We want to tell him about our cache of electronic parts."

"We should try to find a complete map of the base tomorrow," said George. "Then we can start locating everybody on it."

When Carol returned from her watch, she said that she had contacted eight more. They now knew where twenty eight of the hundred were staying.

"We had a successful day today," said Nancy with a smile.

They turned on their TV later that night. After the news broadcast they watched a show that was meant to be entertainment

"Their music sounds strange," said Janet.

"You can tell it is a love song, though," said Gayle. "The men and women use the approach or mannerisms that one would use in a love song."

"Yes, that last one was a love song," said Nancy. "I even translated one of their sentences in it, and it used their word for love."

The next morning after breakfast, Nancy and Carl set off to meet Albert Haynes in his building. Carl carried the bag of electronic parts he had found in the junk yard.

George and the three girls decided to go to the bookstore to see if they could locate a complete map of the base.

George said, "You know, one of us has to get some kind of a job so we can get one of those charge cards."

"Yes," answered Carol. "We might be here a whole year. We will want to be able to buy things."

"It would have to be a job where we don't do much talking," said Carol.

"One of us could learn enough of the Philadelphian language by using Nancy's dictionary," said Janet, "to apply for a job moving goods around in a warehouse. Nancy said that she and Carl had practiced the Philadelphian language quite a bit once. Maybe they could fill out the form and Carl could apply for the job."

Carol said, "Let's go into one of these warehouses and see if there is some kind of a form on a table that looks like a job application form. We can take it home and fill it out."

They digressed from their path to the bookstore to go in search of a warehouse.

"Here's one," said George. "I'll just walk in and look around. I won't try to talk to anyone."

He came out a few minutes later with three forms. "I don't know if any of these are job application forms," said George. "They were just lying on a table."

They resumed their trip to the bookstore. When they arrived, they entered and strolled about for about an hour.

"They have all kinds of books from earth," said Carol. "Some people on the base must know French, English, or German."

"I noticed some maps of the base in a dispenser," said Gayle. "But you need a card to buy them."

While George and Carol were visiting warehouses and the library, Nancy and Carl went over to Albert Haynes and Charles Richardson's living space. They found Albert Haynes and Charles Richardson in their building without any trouble. Carl showed Albert the bag of electronic parts.

"There are probably more parts in that junk yard," said Carl. "We could go back and look."

"This is a good start," said Albert Haynes.

"Did you notice any cell phones lying about?" asked Charles Richardson.

"Yes," answered Nancy. "We have one but we are afraid that if we start using it, the Philadelphians might intercept our message."

"I just thought that if we got off to the edge of the carrier band, they might not notice us," answered Albert.

"Could you convert these cell phones into walkie-talkies?" asked Nancy.

"We would have to change the circuitry to do that," answered Albert. "I'll check into it. In the mean time, try to find some more discarded cell phones. If we have twelve, altogether, that should be enough."

When they got back to their building, George and the girls were already there.

"We found the maps at the bookstore," said Gayle, "but you have to buy them with a card."

"I went into one of the warehouses to see if I could find an application form for work," said George. "Can you translate any of these forms, Nancy, using your dictionary?"

Nancy looked at them and discovered that one was a job application form. "I'll get my dictionary and translate it completely."

After a short time, Nancy said, "It is an application for a man to work in the warehouse. He takes things off the loading dock and puts them on shelves. Also, he takes things from the shelves and fills orders."

"I can do that," said Carl. "Nancy and I have been practicing the Philadelphian language for years. I can speak it a little. I think I should apply for the job."

"OK," said George.

"Let's fill out the form, Carl," said Nancy.

They spent about an hour filling out the form and Carl decided to go to the warehouse the next day and apply for the job.

"I can answer a few questions in their language," said Carl. "It should go all right."

At noon the next day, Carl returned to their building and announced jubilantly, "I got the job. I work Tuesday mornings from 8 am till noon."

"Congratulations, Carl," said Nancy.

"Good for you," said George.

"I have my card already," said Carl, "but there is probably no money in my account yet."

"But there will be next Wednesday," said Janet with a grin.

The next day they set out for more groceries and another stop at the junk yard. They found some more plates and pots for the kitchen.

Janet said, "Gayle, let's hunt for some discarded boxes of soap. I might even be able to find a new tooth brush; mine is almost worn out."

"OK," said Gayle.

After rooting around in boxes and cartons Nancy found several cell phones in their original boxes. "Look at this, Carl," she said. "I found four brand new cell phones. They haven't even been removed from their boxes."

"Great," said Carl. "Maybe, there are some electronic parts nearby."

After a short search they found several boxes of condensers, resistors, transformers, circuit boards, and transistors. "I wonder why they throw so much stuff away," said Carl.

They climbed over the fence and returned home.

The next Tuesday, Carl set off for work at the warehouse.

Carl reported to his foreman, Mr. Radol, as directed.

Mr. Radol said, "Carl, you will work with Zardol today. A shipment of building materials will arrive at dock 2 in about an hour."

"Yes, sir," responded Carl.

Carl said hello to Zardol. Since Carl didn't know many Philadelphian words, he didn't try to engage Zardol in any lengthy conversation. Fortunately, Zardol took a book from his pocket and sat in the corner, against the wall, to read until the shipment arrived. When it arrived, Carl and Zardol stacked the new materials on the appropriate shelves.

The morning went fast and Carl went home at noon. Upon inserting his card in a card reading machine on the way home, Carl discovered that he finally had some money in his account.

Upon entering their living quarters in their building, Carl announced, "We have money folks. We can buy some things."

"Hurray," shouted Nancy.

"Let's get a map at the book store," said Carl. "And then we can look at other things."

They all set out after lunch. They went to the book store and purchased the map without any difficulty.

"I wonder how fast we would go through the money if we stopped at one of these restaurants," said Gayle.

"Very fast," said Janet.

"Should we visit a real grocery store?" asked Carol.

They all agreed. After about an hour they returned home with their purchases and turned on the TV.

"Nothing out of the ordinary on TV," said Janet. "Another war is raging on earth in Asia."

Carl said he was going over to Albert Haynes and Charles Richardson's building with the new map and electronic parts and cell phones.

Albert and Charles lived in building 15. Carl entered the door in the back which was never locked and went up the stairs to the third floor. He knocked on the door of a room way at the back. Albert looked out through a peek hole and then opened the door

"Well, how is the working man?" asked Charles with a grin.

"Just fine," answered Carl. "I bought an official map of the base at the book store," he said, laying the map on the table.

They immediately started perusing the map.

"I also got some more electronic parts," said Carl, placing his bag on the table. "Here are four new cell phones," he added.

"I have been studying the circuit board of the cell phone you gave me the other day," said Albert Haynes. "I think we can alter the carrier frequency enough so that they won't detect us when we use the cell phone."

"Have we enough radio parts to do it?" asked Carl.

"Yes," answered Albert, "I think so."

"I'll make a card out showing the building number of each group," said Charles. "Then we can locate everyone on the map."

"How many groups do we know about now?" asked Carl.

"We have contacted twelve groups so far, and that's everybody," answered Charles. "We know where everybody is living."

"Is everyone getting enough to eat?" asked Carl.

"Yes," said Albert. "That has worked out smoothly."

"When do you think you will have the cell phones ready for a trial run, Albert?" asked Carl.

"In a few days," answered Albert. "I have the wire to wind coils for a slightly different frequency. I have a soldering iron. I've got lots of capacitors and resistors. I should have it ready in a few days."

"You and Charles can test two of the cell phones here," said Carl, "after you've made the changes."

"Yes, that's true," answered Albert.

"Have you people noticed how many shuttles come and go to earth?" asked Carl.

"I've been keeping track," answered Charles.

"There seems to be a departure from Titan every Tuesday and Friday and an arrival on Titan every Wednesday and Saturday," said Charles.

"That's pretty good," said Carl.

"Once we are ready," said Albert, "all one hundred of us should be able to get out of here in just one and a half months."

"Sounds totally excellent," exclaimed Carl. "Well, I'll be off and keep in touch."

"Stop back in three days," said Albert. "I might have our cell phone communication system working."

"OK," said Carl. "We will also search for more cell phones in the junk yard. Did you say that there are twelve groups?"

"Yes, twelve groups," answered Charles.

When Carl returned to his building he relayed the promising news about the cell phones."

"So, there are about eight shuttles leaving here every month," said George. "That's good news."

"There must be a lot of shuttles in motion to maintain that level of traffic," said Nancy.

Carl adjusted to his Tuesday morning work schedule quite easily. He and Zardol got along well. Zardol was totally engrossed in his books. Carl asked him a few questions about the stories and decided that Zardol was a science fiction fan.

One nice thing about the job was that Carl got paid every Tuesday. That is, his card account had money added to it every Tuesday.

# Chapter 14

When Carl arrived at Albert Haynes and Charles Richardson's building later that week they were very pleased with themselves.

"We don't think the Philadelphians are aware of our ever having used their cell phone network," said Charles.

"That's great," said Carl. "I brought along seven more cell phones that we found. That makes twelve altogether. So, each group will have a cell phone."

"We have plenty of electronic parts," said Albert. "I can get all twelve to work."

"Could I take one of your converted cell phones with me?" asked Carl. "Then we can check them out at a distance."

"Sure," said Albert. "Take this one."

"I have entered our number in the frequently called list. It is called USA. Don't call the other numbers."

"Right," said Carl. "I'll leave now and call you in about half an hour."

"OK," said Charles.

Carl went straight home. The possibility of private conversations between the Californians without the Philadelphians listening in was satisfying. More than that, it was essential. When Carl entered their rooms, all five were there.

Carl held up the cell phone and said, "Albert Haynes just set up our communications system. I am going to try it."

He dialed USA and waited for the ring.

"Hello," answered Albert.

"Hi, Albert," said Carl. "This is Carl. It works fine. Are you pretty sure there is no way the Philadelphians can listen in on our phone conversation?"

"I am not absolutely certain," said Albert. "But we are way off on the end of the frequency band. It is extremely unlikely that they would be hunting around out there."

"But is it possible?" asked Carl.

"It is possible," answered Albert. "You see, their transmitter establishes the carrier frequency. We can't alter that. We can only get way off on the edge of the band where they are not likely to go"

"OK," said Carl. "I guess we have no choice."

"We could make walkie-talkies out of these cell phones and thereby establish our own carrier frequency." said Albert. "But that would require a lot of new circuit board wiring. We would have to make crystal controlled oscillators for each cell phone. We might not even have the parts."

"OK," said Carl. "Let it go. We'll just hope they don't periodically traverse the band in search of foreign traffic."

"We are going to have to get over to the hanger where they load the shuttles and devise a way to board those things without being seen."

"Yes," said Albert. "We will watch the shuttles closely and find out where they are loaded."

"Charles Richardson said the other day that Colonel Smith was in a room with a good view of the landing facility," said Carl.

"Yes," said Albert. "I heard that also. Charles and I will contact Colonel Smith and arrange for a meeting. We can also give him a cell phone at that time."

About a week later, Charles Richardson called Carl to inform him of a meeting that had been arranged with the Colonel. After work on the following Tuesday, Carl and Nancy went over to Albert Haynes and Charles Richardson's building. The four of them set off for building 9, where Colonel Smith lived.

"Hello, everybody," said Colonel Smith when he opened the door.

"Hi," said Nancy. They all trooped in.

Colonel Smith opened a small window on one wall of his room; it afforded an excellent view of the loading zone and warehouse complex.

"Have you figured out which warehouse is used to load and unload the shuttles?" asked Carl.

"It is the big one in the center with the number 11 on it," answered Colonel Smith.

"Maybe we should go down there the day before a departure and just watch the procedure," said Charles.

"Sounds like a good idea," said Colonel Smith.

"When is the next departure?" asked Charles. "Do you know?"

"Just a minute," said the Colonel, reaching for a paper in a drawer. "I have been keeping a schedule. It should be next Friday."

"Suppose we meet here next Wednesday night," said Nancy. "We can go down there and get in the building during the night and then watch the loading process on Thursday."

"Fine," said Colonel Smith.

Albert handed Colonel Smith his cell phone and they left. When they got back to their building the subject of which group should depart first for earth came up.

"There are twelve groups," said Carol, "but they are not all the same size. They probably average about eight people per group."

"There will be about eight departures per month," said Carl, "according to the schedule we have been keeping."

"So we send eight groups the first month and four groups the second month," said George.

"Now all that has to be decided is the order of the groups," said Gayle.

"Suppose a representative from each group meets at Colonel Smith's building," said Carl, "and they draw straws."

"I don't think we should let the panicky ones stay to the end," said Nancy. "They should be sent after the first group."

"I think you are right," said Carl.

"OK," said George. "We will bring it up Wednesday night."

After supper, Janet thought of something. "Do you suppose they found the spaceship we used to escape from the Dynasty?"

"Oh, my," said Nancy. "I forgot about that."

"With establishing our new living quarters here we completely forgot about that spaceship," said Gayle.

"We parked it right near building 9 didn't we?" asked Carl.

"Yes," said George.

"We could go over there tonight and see if it is still there," said Carl.

"Why?" said Janet. "We are not going to use it. Why run the risk?"

"If they found it," said George, "they will be looking for us. It gives us an idea of how intently they are looking for us."

"We can go over to building 9 and look around," said Carl. "But we probably shouldn't go right up to it. They might have rigged it with an alarm if they found it."

"Or, they could have surveillance cameras all over the place," said Gayle.

"That's a thought," interjected George.

"Let's just go up to about a hundred yards of it," said Carl.

"But what can we deduce from that?" asked Carol. "They would probably leave it right there even if they had gone on board."

"I'm beginning to think we have nothing to gain from going there," said Gayle.

"I tend to agree," said Carl.

"There is one thing, though," said George. "If they found the spaceship and determine Californians were aboard, then they will watch the space shuttle carefully. Whereas, if they think Dynasty people were on board, then they will watch their military factories."

"Yes," said Carl. "That's a good point."

"Let's just assume," said Nancy, "that if they find the spaceship, they will deduce that Californians were aboard. Someone of us probably dropped a piece of paper on the floor with an English word on it."

"Right," said Carl.

On Wednesday they got ready to go down to Colonel Smith's building. Nancy and Carl, George and Carol, Janet, and Gayle set out after supper for Colonel Smith's building.

"I made plenty of sandwiches," said Nancy. "I made ham and cheese sandwiches and also beef sandwiches. We might have to be in that warehouse all day Thursday."

"I made a big box of sliced apples, pears, and oranges," said Carol.

"I've got a gallon jug of water," said George.

"Did you bring along the binoculars, Carl?" asked Nancy.

"Yes," answered Carl.

They got to Colonel Smith's building about 7 pm. When Colonel Smith opened his door, he said, "Hello, everybody. I see you brought lunches for tomorrow. That's showing good foresight."

"At what time do the workers usually go home from the warehouses?" asked Carl.

"I've noticed in the past that they are all usually gone by 6 pm," said Colonel Smith.

"They stay around later if a spaceship is being loaded and is scheduled to leave the next morning."

"In our case," said George, "the ship is going back to earth relatively empty on Friday."

"So, the workers in our warehouse should be gone by 6 pm tonight and Thursday," said Nancy.

"As soon as it gets dark, we will go over tonight," said Colonel Smith.

They left Colonel Smith's room at 9 pm. The streets were pretty much deserted. Nancy counted six warehouses in the area. Each warehouse was a two story building with few windows. Just outside each warehouse was a large loading area for a spaceship. A few lights were located in the edges of the warehouse roofs and also there were a few street lights. The space shuttle to earth was standing outside building 11 with its landing lights on. The space shuttle was a large ship. It was shaped like an ellipsoid with a length of about 500 feet, width of about 300 feet, and height of about 50 feet. They went up to building 11 and tried the door.

"Good, the door is unlocked," said Colonel Smith. "I brought my lock picks just in case."

They entered quietly and looked around.

"Nobody is here," said George.

"Let's look around and find out what they are going to load tomorrow," said Carl.

"Looks like most of these packing crates are empty," said Janet.

"Yes," answered George. "They are brought here full from earth and sent back to earth empty for the next load."

"There are some very large plastic cases in the middle of the floor," said Gayle. "Do you suppose they bring large prefabricated pieces or sections of a spaceship in them?"

"It looks like it," said Carl. "They could design a spaceship up here on Titan and then have the sub-assemblies made on earth."

"We shouldn't have much trouble hiding in these empty crates," said Janet. "Then they would just carry us out from the warehouse here and put us on the space shuttle."

"It might not be necessary to do it that way," said Carl. "We could walk out right now and climb aboard that space shuttle parked on the loading strip."

"Yes," said Colonel Smith. "It is dark out there except for a few lights."

"Should we go upstairs and find our vantage places for viewing the loading operation tomorrow?" asked George.

"I want to go over to that small office by the gate," said Colonel Smith. "The loading schedule for tomorrow might be there."

"Yes," said George. "That way we will know the order of events for tomorrow."

They walked over to the office and went in. As usual, nothing was locked. They noticed a computer on a desk. Nancy sat down and started searching the documents.

"Here is the record of what arrived on the last shuttle," Nancy said. "It looks like a list of fuselage walls and passage ways. The outer skin is a type of aluminum alloy. Here are some nuclear reactor parts. Oh, here are the food and clothing consignments. Finally, here is a long list of electronic components."

"I found tomorrow's loading schedule," said Colonel Smith. "They will start at 7:30 am and finish at 4 pm. It gives the times that they will carry out each of those empty packing crates."

"Well, let's go upstairs and look around," said Colonel Smith.

They found a stair case to the second floor of the warehouse and went up. As they were proceeding, Colonel Smith said, "This building, as well as the one I live in, are made with light weight metal beams for structural strength and then a grey plastic or vinyl covering is put on it. Nothing is very heavy so they don't need much if any steel reinforcement."

"That was probably dictated by the fact that they would have to bring any heavy steel up on the space shuttle," said George.

"Yes, everything is pretty flimsy," said Carl, "except for the center shell of this station. Remember there are walls and a cover over the top to protect against the extreme cold."

"Titan is a huge moon," put in George, "so it will have a substantial field of gravity."

"Yes," said Carl, "so you don't want to have too much mass in the structure."

"Like I said," put in the Colonel, "the structures have strong light weight metal reinforcement bars and very light vinyl covering."

They had attained the second floor and were walking across a large central room.

"More empty packing containers," said Gayle.

"Over here is a small room with a window in the wall overlooking the spaceship loading platform," said Janet. She was standing near an outer wall of the building. "We could watch them load the spaceship from the window."

"Just ten feet from where you are standing, Janet, is a staircase leading down," said Gayle. "We could occasionally look down and observe activities on the first floor."

"OK," said Carl. "Let's set up our observation post in that room. I brought a padlock and hasp with me. So, if the Philadelphians try to get into the room while we are there, they won't be able to."

Everyone agreed and they took some empty boxes into the room and set up their living quarters. After having a light supper the subject of the order of departure for the twelve groups was brought up.

"The first group down will have to be fairly resourceful," began Carl. "They will have to get off the spaceship and then get off the base unobserved down there on earth."

"Yes," said George. "We can't have people caught down there. The Philadelphians would send a message up here and a hunt would be made for the remaining people."

"Also," said Colonel Smith, "the last group out has to organize all of the departures and make sure no one gets overly excited or alarmed that they might not get out."

"Nancy and I thought," put in Carl, "that it would be fair if we drew straws to determine the order of departure."

"That would be OK," said Colonel Smith. "However, I think we should make an exception for the first and last groups out."

"Do you mean pick the first and last groups for the reasons just mentioned," said Gayle, "but choose all the other departures by drawing straws?"

"Yes," answered Colonel Smith.

"That's OK with me," said Carl.

"Yes, that's fine with me," said George.

"OK, who goes first and last?" asked Gayle.

"I suggest," said Colonel Smith, "that you six people constitute the first group out. Albert Haynes, Charles Richardson, and I will go out with the last group."

"That sounds OK," said Carl. "Nobody else is in on that decision, which might not be that fair."

"I don't think they will balk or complain," said Gayle. "They have accepted our lead thus far."

"So, we can notify the other groups to have a representative go to Colonel Smith's building sometime in the next two weeks and pick a number, between 2 and 11, out of a hat," said George.

"I have been in contact with all the groups," said Colonel Smith. "So I will pass the message."

"Have those cell phones modified by Albert Haynes been very helpful?" asked Janet.

"Very," answered Colonel Smith.

The next morning they were up early to observe the loading operation.

"I count twenty workers in the warehouse and two others in the space shuttle," said George soon after the operation began.

"Yes," said Janet. "The two inside the space shuttle are just inside that big rear door of the space ship that must be the loading bay."

"There is probably a ramp under that door that can come down to the ground when they are loading full boxes," said Janet. "They just don't need the ramp down to load these empty boxes."

"Notice that two men go out on those little motorized carts from the warehouse," said Colonel Smith, "that carry the crates up to the ship's hold."

"I was thinking last night," said Gayle, "about how we are to get aboard that space shuttle. What if they lock the space shuttle after they load it?"

"Yes, the trouble is that the key to open it might be a radio signal," said Carl.

"We wouldn't be able to pick the lock," continued George.

"I was watching the working crews carefully," said Carl, "and keeping track of where each crew member was at all times. I noticed that the two loading crew members who worked inside the spaceship entered through the cockpit door in the front and then went to the back loading ramp."

"Did they close the cockpit door?" asked George.

"That is what I was leading up to," answered Carl. "They didn't close it. Furthermore, none of the loading crew members who worked in the warehouse went near it all morning."

"So, one of us could get in through the front cockpit door without being seen," said Nancy.

"Exactly," said Carl.

"And if he stayed hidden all day," said the Colonel, "he could let the other group members in during the night."

"Even if the loading crew that works aboard the ship closed the front cockpit door upon entering," said George, "they wouldn't lock it behind them."

"There would be no reason to," said Gayle. "They would figure they were the only people at the warehouse."

"I think that solves it," said Carl. "We have our way of entering the space shuttle."

By noon the loading crew had completely loaded the space shuttle with the empty cargo crates.

"This after noon, they will probably service the space ship," said the Colonel. "That would entail servicing the nuclear reactor engines and all the electronic systems on the spaceship."

"At least they don't have to refuel the ship," said Janet.

"Oh, no" said the Colonel. "The reactor fuel rods are good for years."

"There is a lengthy check list before take off of a standard jet airplane," said George. "So, there must also be a long check list for a ship like this."

At four o'clock the space shuttle was loaded and the Philadelphian workers were getting ready to leave. The lights in the warehouse were turned off. Only the lights on the roof and on the spaceship were left on.

Carl and Nancy and the others left at 8 pm.

Colonel Smith remarked, "It doesn't look like too difficult of an operation for us."

"No, it looks pretty easy," said George. "The only tricky part is getting one of our group members into the front cockpit door during the morning."

"That shouldn't be too hard," said Gayle. "He can dress the same way as the loading crew members."

When they got back to Colonel Smith's building, they made supper and discussed the day's activities. Colonel Smith had a supper of roast chicken and potatoes.

"Isn't it amazing how they bring all the grand food out to this moon?" said Carol.

"Yes," answered Janet. "I guess the Philadelphians have gotten to like our kind of food."

"We could turn on the TV and see what the Philadelphian latest news is," said George.

"OK," said Colonel Smith.

He turned it on to the only station the Philadelphians had. The TV announcer came on and reported the news of the day. All the Californians on Titan had learned enough of the Philadelphian language to understand ordinary conversation used on the street and in the stores.

"Our Three Year Plan," began the announcer, "is on schedule. We have completed the construction of ten spaceships. We have designed and completed the construction of our communication system. We can now maintain contact between all of our spaceships and also with those Philadelphians who remained on our planet in Alpha Centauri. Of course, it takes 4 years to exchange an idea, but it works in principal."

He continued, "The people on earth are trying to end their current war. They have at least reduced the level of fighting."

"By the way, Colonel," said Carl, "did you find out how many of the Philadelphians returned here after their battle with the Barstonians?"

"We have figured out," said Colonel Smith, "that most of them managed to get back. Only a few were taken prisoner."

"Did you and Charles Richardson work that out by analyzing radio broadcasts?" asked Carl.

"Yes," answered Colonel Smith. "We used their radio and TV broadcasts and figured that approximately 95% of them returned here after their aborted attack on the Dynasty. Only about 5% of that armada are prisoners in New Barstow."

During the next two weeks a representative of each of the remaining ten groups went to the building where Colonel Smith was living. The representative reached into a hat held by Colonel Smith and pulled out a paper with a number printed on it.

Colonel Smith then explained that the first group consisted of Carl Johnson, Nancy Jones, George Erickson, Carol Chandler, Janet Snyder, and Gayle Poitiers.

He then told the representative that the twelfth group consisted of himself, Albert Haynes, Charles Richardson, and five Californians.

He mentioned that the first group would be the first to go back to earth on the space shuttle, and that his twelfth group would be the last.

Colonel Smith stated that since the twelfth group would be the last group to leave, he would be on Titan to coordinate the departure of all the groups. He stated that since he was near the warehouse where the space shuttle is loaded, he would know on what days the shuttles departed and would therefore notify each group which day to be ready.

He went on to say that a departing group would go to warehouse 11 at about 8 pm on the evening before their spaceship would be loaded. They would then go to the room on the second floor where a lock and key had been installed for their benefit.

Colonel Smith told the group representative that the empty crates would be loaded onto the space shuttle during the day by the loading crews. He said that two loading crew members enter the space ship from the front but work in the back all morning. Therefore, one of the Californians must enter the front cockpit unseen and hide in the space ship all day. That person could let the others in during the following night. Colonel

Smith emphasized that great care must be taken by the Californian to not be seen when entering the cockpit in the morning.

Colonel Smith then went on to say that all the loading crew members go home around 4 pm. He said that there are many places in the cargo bay of the space shuttle where the group could hide during the trip.

Colonel Smith said finally that the disembarking procedure on earth would be easy. The space shuttle doors all open from the inside even if the flight crew is gone. He said the first group to return to earth would stay in the vicinity of the earth landing zone and provide a means of transportation back to a city.

After breakfast one morning Nancy said to Carl, "I think we should go to the junk yard or the stores and buy some uniforms like the warehouse loaders use."

"Are you afraid that the Californian, who approaches the front cockpit door, might be stopped and interrogated?" asked Carl.

"Yes, that could happen," answered Nancy.

"It is possible," allowed Carl, "that one of the two Philadelphian loaders inside the space shuttle might go to the cockpit for some reason."

"Or maybe one of the twenty Philadelphian loaders assigned to the warehouse might look out a window and see him," said Nancy.

"OK," answered Carl, "we can go buy some clothes."

"Do you have enough money from your Tuesday job?" asked Nancy.

"Yes, I have quite a bit," answered Carl.

"We might have to buy only one set of clothes or uniform," said Nancy. "The person who enters the cockpit can leave the uniform in our little room in the warehouse later that night for the next group of Californians."

"Yes," answered Carl.

"There is usually a badge on the cap of uniforms," said Nancy, "or an insignia on the shoulder of the shirt. How can we find those things?"

"We could go over to that warehouse next Thursday and take photographs of the cap and shirt," said Carl.

"Yes, that would work," said Nancy. "Just the two of us could go."

"We will go Wednesday night and stay in that little room in the warehouse," said Carl. "We will take our camera along and take the pictures the next day."

"Colonel Smith said that the space shuttle leaves every Tuesday and Friday," said Nancy.

"OK, let's go over next Wednesday night," said Carl.

Accordingly, Nancy and Carl went to warehouse 11 the next Wednesday night. They had their camera and the key to the little room on the second floor. They stole quietly down the staircase the next morning and spent some time observing the workers in the warehouse.

Nancy whispered, "They all wear the same uniform."

Carl whispered back, "We will just pick the person who is easiest for us to photograph."

"Make sure the flash button is turned OFF," said Nancy.

Carl double checked and said, "It is."

Carl and Nancy were hiding behind some packing crates along the wall. During the next half hour, they took photographs of the hat, shirt, pants, and shoes of three different workers who passed near them. Soon after the warehouse loaders left at 4 pm to go home, Carl and Nancy left.

Carl said, "We can buy the shirt, pants, and shoes in the stores. I have seen them before."

"Yes, but the insignia and badge are another thing," said Nancy.

"We will have to carefully make them," said Carl. "We can buy several small pieces of colored cloth to make the insignia."

"We can make the badge from a piece of metal that we ought to be able to find in the junk yard," said Nancy.

"Yes," answered Carl. "Both the badge and insignia will require a little artistic ability."

"There is a store that sells colored scarves and decorative ornaments for clothing on that main shopping street," said Nancy.

"OK, let's go to that store first and buy what we can," said Carl. "What we can't buy maybe we can find in the junk yard."

Carl bought the shirt, pants, and shoes with no difficulty. He used their photographs to make the correct selections. When they got to the store with colored scarves, they stood outside for a few moments and examined their photographs.

"We need these shades of red, blue, and yellow," said Nancy, pointing at the photographs. "Why don't you stay out here and I will go in and see what I can find."

Fifteen minutes later, Nancy came out with a bag and said, "I got it."

They proceeded to the junk yard and scaled the fence. They found a suitable piece of scrap tin a short time later.

"I am satisfied with this piece of tin," said Carl. "I can make the badge from it using the tin snips we have in our tool box. We have a very nice tool box now. I found all kinds of great tools at the junk yard and bought some as well."

When they returned home, they began assembling their warehouse uniform. It took them several hours over two days to finish it.

"It looks quite authentic," said Nancy.

"I agree," said Carl.

"What our Californian needs, in addition to his uniform, is some suitable statement to make if he is intercepted in the cockpit," said Nancy.

"We can compose the statement in the Philadelphian language," said Carl, "if we can come up with a convincing excuse for his being there."

"Well, he could say that he was just going to the spaceship storage space to see how the work was progressing," said Nancy.

"Yes, that might work," said Carl. "He has no proper business in the cockpit area; so, he can't say that he has to check the controls or documents there."

"We will have him make a remark about the big and unwieldy packing crates," said Nancy.

"OK," agreed Carl.

So, Nancy composed the statement in proper Philadelphian syntax. She threw in a few complaining words about the heavy work load to make it sound genuine.

"I think we are in pretty good shape for this entire enterprise," said Carl.

"I agree," said Nancy.

"Should we go over to Colonel Smith's building tomorrow and say we are ready?" asked Carl. "We can take along our uniform."

"Sure, we're ready," said Nancy.

The next night, Carl and Nancy, along with the other members of their group, went over to Colonel Smith's building.

Colonel Smith answered the door. "Hello, Nancy, and everybody," he said.

Albert Haynes and Charles Richardson and the rest of Colonel Smith's group were there.

"Hi," returned Nancy.

"First, we have to show you, Colonel Smith, our glorious uniform," said Nancy. "Carl and I made it."

Carl had gone into the bathroom and came out dressed in the uniform. Nancy provided a little fan fare for the event by whistling and a little singing.

"Nancy and I photographed the workers at the loading warehouse last week," said Carl, "and then made this uniform for our guy who goes to the cockpit door."

"Give him the statement," said Nancy.

Carl said, "Here is the excuse he can give if he is observed in the cockpit."

Carl stated the excuse in proper Philadelphian language. "Nancy composed the statement," said Carl.

"Whoever uses the uniform to get into the space ship can leave the uniform in our little room later that night for the next group," said Nancy.

Colonel Smith's group congratulated Carl and Nancy on their achievement.

Then Carl said, "Our group is ready to go."

"We can leave our belongings for the other groups," said Nancy.

"We can leave our card also," said Carl. "It still has quite a bit of monetary value left in it."

"Well, we appreciate that," said Colonel Smith.

"By the way, has anyone else in the groups been able to get a job?" asked Carl.

"Yes," answered Colonel Smith. "Altogether, nine people are working part time," answered Colonel Smith.

"I think we are ready to put our plan into motion," said Charles Richardson.

"Everything has been checked and discussed," added Albert Haynes.

"Yes," said Colonel Smith, "everyone in all the groups is in agreement with the plan."

"It would be nice if you could send a message back to us after you arrive on earth," said Albert Haynes. "But that doesn't seem possible."

"All right," said Colonel Smith. "Let's begin our space shuttle plan starting next Thursday."

"Your entire group," said Colonel Smith gesturing towards Carl, Nancy, George, Carol, Janet, and Gayle, "should be down at warehouse 11 next Wednesday night. I'll come along as an observer."

Everybody was silent for a few moments, thinking of the importance of making this final move.

After packing up the uniform, Nancy and Carl and their entire group walked back to their building.

Carl and Nancy spent the next few days saying goodbye to the remaining groups. Nancy had bought an attractive handbag at one of the stores and spent some time deciding which of her possessions to put in it. She certainly wouldn't take any of the kitchen utensils, no matter how utilitarian they were. Besides, they came from the US via the space shuttle anyway. She put her notebook in the hand bag. She had hundreds of little notes and reminders in that notebook. She put her camera with its pictures in the bag. Some of her prize items were two figurines and a small purse she had bought on the New Barstow base. These went into the handbag.

Nancy and Carl and the others set out from their living quarters at 8 pm, Wednesday. Janet and Gayle were as happy as one could be. George and Carol were slightly apprehensive.

"How are we going to select the person who will enter the cockpit?" asked George.

"I have been practicing the lines that can be said in the cockpit if necessary," said Carl, "but I have noticed that you are more simpatico and have the Philadelphian diction down very well."

"If the person who enters the cockpit is challenged," said George, "it would be advantageous to be able to make small talk."

"I think you're right," said Carl. "How do you feel about taking the job?"

"I think I can handle it quite well," said George. "I watched the Philadelphian warehouse workers when we were here before. I know what their job consists of—what they are moving and so forth—and I have listened to their friendly talk amongst themselves."

"Do you want to do it then?" asked Carl.

"Sure, I'll take the job," said George.

When they got to building 11, they found the door open as usual. Carl had brought his lock pick just in case. Colonel Smith met them inside the building; he had mentioned that he wanted to observe the departure. They quietly went to their second floor room. They used their padlock and key to lock the door from the inside. It was always possible that when the warehouse workers arrived in the morning, they might inspect the premises. They hung the uniform up on a wall peg to preserve its pressed appearance.

"Carol and I brought a lunch basket," said Nancy, "with enough for our group for several days. Should we have some now?"

"Sure," said Carl.

As they all sat down to sandwiches and drinks, Nancy asked, "Does the trip from Saturn to Earth take about three days?"

"Yes, as I recall," said George. "That is about right."

"Is this a peanut butter and jelly sandwich?" asked Gayle in amazement.

"Yes," answered Nancy. "A lot of American favorites have been taken up to Titan by the shuttles."

"I see from your lunch basket," said Janet, "that a large selection of soft drinks have been included."

"Oh, that is certainly true," answered Carol and Nancy.

"I wonder how delicate of a maneuver it will be to get off this space ship on earth," said George.

"Well the American military knows this shuttle operation is going on," said Carl. "But, it is not supposed to be common knowledge."

"I can't remember now," said Janet. "Were there a lot of lights on around the landing field at night?"

"As I recall, there were quite a few lights," said Carl, "but they weren't bright lights."

"The highway is about a mile and a half away," added George, "but there is no town for a long ways. The nearest one is about 30 miles away."

"If we are lucky, there will be a lot of clutter at the base," put in Nancy. "Maybe, a lot of packing crates will be near the landing site."

"There are only empty packing crates on this ship," said Carl. "There probably won't be any big rush to unload this space ship."

"I don't think we will encounter much trouble," said Nancy.

Janet and Gayle were looking out the little window that was in the outer wall of the room they were in.

"Well there is our ride home," said Gayle, referring to the space shuttle parked on the pad just outside the warehouse.

"Nice, old friendly airplane," purred Janet.

"It has number A317 on its tail or rudder sticking up in the back," said Gayle.

"Why do you think it is painted white?" asked Janet.

"To reflect the sun light, I suppose," said Gayle. "Maybe it could absorb a lot of heat in direct sunlight if it didn't reflect it with white paint."

"This spaceship is pretty big, isn't it?" asked Janet.

"Yes," answered Gayle. "It has a lot of freight to haul up here every month."

"I wonder," said Janet. "Do you think this space ship can get up to nine tenths the speed of light like the one we used between here and Alpha Centauri?"

"I don't know," answered Gayle. "It is not the same model, is it?"

"No, this one is longer and fatter," said Janet with a smile.

"They all use nuclear reactors," said Gayle. "But that doesn't mean, I suppose, that they can all go the same speed."

"What speeds did Charles Richardson say that the Titan to Alpha Centauri ship could go?" asked Janet.

"Didn't he say it could go at nine tenths the speed of light or slow down to 30,000 miles per hour?"

"Yes," said Gayle, "that sounds right. So, maybe this one can go 30,000 miles per hour."

"It seems funny to look at one of these and see windows only in the front," said Gayle. "Of course, they don't carry passengers, just a crew."

"I imagine they have viewing sensors placed all over the outside," said Janet. "There must be TV screens in the cockpit so the pilot can see what the viewing sensors are pointing at."

"Most of the spaceships that I've seen so far have this same ellipsoidal shape," said Gayle. "Do you suppose that enables them to move easily through atmosphere when they approach a planet?"

"Could be," said Janet. "An ellipsoidal shape would cut down on air friction."

"You know, I can't see any great big exhaust funnels, like on a jet," said Gayle.

"Yes, I have thought about that also," said Janet. "What if they have great big coils inside the space ship where they pass electric current? And then these coils cause a magnetic field which reacts with the magnetic fields in space."

"You think this magnetic reaction provides the propulsion through space?" asked Gayle.

"It might be," answered Janet.

"The magnetic field in space must be pretty weak in most places," said Gayle.

"Yes, you are probably right," said Janet.

"But they can't throw off mass all the time like a jet engine," said Gayle. "They would run out of piles of mass to eject."

"Of course if even a very small amount of mass is given an enormous velocity," said Janet, "it world have substantial momentum, I guess."

"Wow," said Gayle, "enough of this scientific day dreaming from high school teachers and nurses."

They joined the others in the middle of the room.

"So, what have you girls been discussing at the window?" asked George.

"We were working the transportation problem," said Gayle.

"Do any of you know if the spaceship outside can get up to nine tenths the speed of light?" asked Janet.

"Probably not," answered George. "I think they have two models. One is the high speed military model for intragalactic transportation and the other is the lowly cargo ship like the one parked outside."

Carol got out the deck of cards and asked, "Any one for pinochle?"

Several groaned, but said OK.

George and Carl discussed the use of their cell phones tomorrow.

"You will be inside the spaceship tomorrow," said Carl. "Do you think that if you use your cell phone, it will set off some kind of an alarm?"

"Well, there is a lot of sophisticated equipment in there," said George.

"Maybe, we had better not use the cell phones tomorrow," said Carl.

"I concur in that," said Colonel Smith. "We know what everybody is supposed to do. There isn't any need for cell phone communication."

Nancy got up at 7 am. She went to the window and looked out at her last full day on Titan. There were no trees or green grass since the sun light was too weak to support such plant life. Overhead was the plastic dome that allowed the pale light to pass through. No Philadelphians had arrived yet to work on the space shuttle.

Nancy moved over to the wash stand to prepare herself for the day. The running water awakened Carol.

"Good morning, Nancy," said Carol. "Today is a big day for us."

"That's for certain," said Nancy. "I was just thinking that it's our last full day here."

Nancy completed her morning ablutions and moved to the lunch basket. Carol passed to the wash stand as the others began to stir.

Nancy set out the orange juice, cereal, blue berries, strawberries, and put the coffee on. Everybody was cheerful and excited.

"Well, I suppose I can put on my uniform now," said George. "I won't actually go downstairs and put on my charade until around 10 am."

Carl looked out the window and said, "The workers are arriving in their bus now. They are turning off the night lights around the base now as it is getting light outside."

"I decided not to fry bacon or eggs," said Nancy, "because I thought the smell of those might cause the workers to institute a careful search."

"Good idea," remarked Janet.

Everybody used the wash stand and then sat down at the table. Breakfast was very cheerful and expectations were high. They could hear the Philadelphian workers banging around downstairs.

Carol glanced out the window and announced, "The two workers have already gone into the space shuttle. The cockpit door is open in the front."

After breakfast, they sat around and talked about the upcoming flight. From time to time they peered out of their window.

"They are moving the empty packing crates out now," said Gayle. "They're hoisting them up on that hydraulic lift to the spaceship cargo door."

As it approached 10 am, they became more tense and uneasy. Soon George would be going up the portable staircase to the front cockpit door. George was trying to act nonchalant and confident.

At 10 am George picked up his notebook and writing instrument and said, "It is time. I am going to make my play."

Everybody grinned and Carol said, "Good luck, George. We know you're going to succeed."

Carl said, "Be calm, George. Take it easy."

With a smile, George opened the door to the stair and looked down. After a moment he said, "It's clear. I am on my way."

Everybody held their breath. After a minute Carl looked out their window.

"I see him," said Carl. "He is ascending the portable stairs to the cockpit. Nobody is bothering him." After a few seconds, Carl continued, "He just entered the cockpit."

No one made a sound. Every one held their breath.

Carl continued to look out the window. "Everything looks OK. He made it all right."

After a bit, Carol said, "He won't call us on the cell phone. We agreed on that."

After an hour had passed, they started to relax. There was no noticeable change in the warehouse loading procedure. It was proceeding smoothly and there was no change in its pace.

At noon, the loading of packing crates ceased. The loading process was complete.

"They will begin their checkout of the spaceship's flight system now," said Colonel Smith.

"George should be very well hidden by now," said Carl.

The twenty warehouse workers could be heard talking to each other downstairs. The two in the space shuttle were no doubt going through their check list.

As four o'clock rolled around, the group became tense again. They just wanted the whole process to be over without a hitch. Colonel Smith said from the window, "The entire warehouse crew is standing by the gate waiting for the bus." After a few minutes, he continued, "Here comes the bus." After a few more minutes, he said, "Everybody is on board and they're leaving."

Colonel Smith turned his gaze to the space shuttle. "All the spaceship doors are close, and I suppose locked."

They just had to wait for 8 pm to arrive so that they could board the space shuttle.

At 8 pm they saw the front cockpit door open and a rope ladder drop from the cockpit to the ground. They saw George descend the ladder to the ground. The group rushed down the staircase and opened the warehouse door.

"Good job, George," said Colonel Smith. "Did you encounter any difficulties?"

"No, none at all," said George, with a huge smile. "I'll just run upstairs and leave the uniform."

"Your clothes are on the chair," said Carol.

George went up the stairs to their little room, changed his clothes, and was down in a few minutes. Colonel Smith was standing by the warehouse door. The others were all scurrying up the rope ladder to the cockpit.

"Well, everything went great," said Colonel Smith, shaking George's hand. "We will all meet someday in Los Angeles."

"Thank you, sir," said George. "Good luck on the rest of the evacuation."

With that, he hurried to the rope ladder and climbed to the cockpit. He pulled in the rope ladder and shut the cockpit door.

Nancy was waiting in the cockpit. She said, "The others are searching the spaceship for the optimal place to stow away. Where did you spend the day?"

"I was on the second deck," answered George. "There is a small closet or room there for stowing spare parts for the spaceship's electrical system, like fuses and stuff. I locked the door from the inside,"

"We will need a lot more room than that," said Nancy. "Let's go look around."

After a while Carl, met with the others and said, "I found a covered space that goes almost the full length of the ship. It contains circuit breakers for the ship's electrical system and the pipes for the entire plumbing system."

"On what floor is the space?" asked George.

"It is on the second floor," answered Carl. "We could all stay in there. If a crew member started to open the compartment to work on a circuit breaker, we could just move 300 feet down the compartment before he got the compartment open."

"Sounds good," said George.

They all went to the compartment and looked in. It was about 500 feet long, the entire length of the space ship. Although it wasn't very wide it was high enough for a person to stand up in.

"This looks adequate to me," said Carol.

"I agree," said Nancy.

So, they moved into the covered space and make themselves as comfortable as possible.

"Boy, time moves slowly," said Janet, "when you're in position and have nothing to do for the next twelve hours."

"Did any one bring any books?" asked George.

"I have my card decks," said Janet. "We could play bridge if people are tired of pinochle. There is always poker."

Nancy brought out her four paperbacks and said, "I have two classics, a mystery, and a science fiction. Any one interested?"

Two were chosen, leaving one group to play bridge and the others to sit and talk.

"I think Colonel Smith said the shuttle usually lifts off at about 8 am on Fridays," said Carl.

"Yes, I head him say that," responded George.

"I wonder how large the crew is," said Nancy.

"I think Colonel Smith said the crew appeared to consist of 8 people," said George.

"The Colonel certainly has a good vantage point for watching the Philadelphian launch pad," said Carl.

"How do we know that this space we are in will have oxygen to breath once we take off?" asked Nancy.

"Good question," said George with a look of apprehension.

"That was one of the things I checked for when I was looking around," said Carl. "Notice these pipes attached to the wall and running the length of our space. The green pipe is marked every twenty feet with the word oxygen. The black pipe is marked water."

"So, if we need oxygen, we just have to open a little hole in a green pipe," said Nancy.

"All the other spaceships we have been on had passenger rooms," said George, "and we were always put in those rooms."

"But this is a cargo ship," said Carl. "So, we have to check carefully for that."

"Also, it won't get too cold," put in Carol, "because this water pipe would freeze and possibly rupture if it got too cold."

"Right," said Carl. "So, I think we are safe here."

"I wonder if we could tap into these circuit breakers or connection boards and find the pilot's communication link." said Carl. "That way, we could use the ear phones in our cell phones to listen to the crew's conversation."

"Good idea," said George. He opened a connection box and studied the attached wiring diagram. "Too bad Albert Haynes isn't here," he said.

After a few minutes, George said, "I think I found it. Do you have a cell phone?"

Carl handed his cell phone to George.

George used some wire to connect Carl's cell phone to the terminals. "Tomorrow," said George, "I think we will be able to listen in on the crew conversations."

As it was getting late on Thursday night the bridge players decided to quit for the day and try to sleep.

They were awakened Friday morning when the flight crew came aboard.

Carl picked up the cell phone and listened. "They are going through their pre-flight check list," he said.

Gayle came over and asked what was going on.

"The flight crew is aboard and they are running through their pre-flight check list," said Carl.

After about twenty minutes they felt the space shuttle rocking slightly and realized they had lifted off.

"I suppose we are traveling down that long channel to the space portal doors," said Nancy.

"We don't have any window to look out but we do have the pilot's commands," said George.

"He is talking to the space portal door manager now," said George.

After a few moments George said, "We have passed through the doors and have left Titan behind us."

"Well, we are on our three day trip," said Janet. "We might as well relax."

"Fortunately we have four paperback books to pass around," said Gayle.

"Let's start rationing our food," said Nancy. She looked in the lunch basket and started counting. "We are down to thirty four sandwiches, twenty eight pieces of fruit, a bag of raw vegetables, and forty bottles of assorted drinks."

Carol said, "That has to be apportioned among six people over three days. We are going to have to exercise self discipline."

The three days passed slowly. Fortunately, the four books and card decks helped pass the time.

On the third day the crew talk that they heard on the cell phone indicated that the crew had established radio communications with earth. The pilot commenced a periodic flight position adjustment dialog with earth.

Carl said, "We might be there in less than an hour according to this radio traffic."

Everybody became alert and started paying rapt attention to the radio traffic as Carl reported it.

"Earth has us on its radar," said Carl.

After a few minutes, he continued, "Our pilot is adjusting our speed and has entered a flight path for landing."

After another few minutes, Carl announced, "We are right over the landing field and descending."

In a few seconds they felt the space shuttle touch down.

"We have arrived," said Gayle with a huge grin.

"The pilot just stated for the record," said Carl, "that it is 3 pm, Sunday, August 7th, in Barstow, California,"

Carl said a prayer, thanking God for the safe journey.

After a moment of silence, George said, "We will have to sit tight for a few hours. We must wait for the crew to leave and the whole base to quiet down before we dare leave the space shuttle."

The space shuttle was completely silent by 5 pm. Carl said, "I am going to find a window and find out what is going on at the base."

"I will go with you," said Nancy.

They returned after twenty minutes. "We went to the cockpit. You can see all around the base. It is mostly quiet. No trucks are moving. But we saw a few people walking between the buildings."

"Do you think we should wait till dark?" asked George.

"That would probably be a good idea," answered Carl.

"If we go to the pilot cockpit we can see everything and maybe plan our exit path," said Nancy.

They all made their way to the cockpit after first checking to make sure there was no guard or inspector in the cargo hold.

They could see from the cockpit that there was a fence completely surrounding the base and a military guard shack where the road entered the base.

"We can leave the base at the side opposite that guard shack," said Carl.

"We can throw a rug over the barbed wire at the top of the fence," said George, "and use a rope to go up one side of the fence and down the other."

"Those warehouses or storage places over there ought to provide us cover," said Nancy.

"Do you suppose there is a roving guard at night?" asked Carol.

"Yes, probably," answered Carl, "but they would use a jeep with the head lights on."

"It's a long walk from here to the highway," said Janet.

"Yes, but that will be a joyful walk," said Carl.

"OK," said George. "Let's go back and pick up all our debris. Remember we don't want them to find out that there were stowaways. There are eleven more groups to come."

They went back and straightened up their space. Then they all sat down near the cockpit and waited for it to get dark. At 9:15 pm, Carl said that he had been watching through the pilot windows for over an hour and a half and had seen no one.

"Apparently, everyone has gone home except for the guards," he said. "I suppose the Philadelphian flight crew has an apartment or living quarters in a nearby town."

They opened the cockpit door and dropped the rope ladder to the ground. Carl was the last one out. He pulled the rope ladder up, put it in the cabin, and closed the cockpit door. He then jumped to the ground.

They carefully made their way between the warehouse buildings to the back fence. As they advanced they scanned the area to make sure there was no surveillance camera or visual detector mounted on a building. When they got to the fence, they used their shirts to make a pad. Then George scaled the fence and put the pad over the barbed wires. One by one they went over the fence. They retrieved their shirts and were ready to go.

They made a wide detour around the front of the base to avoid being seen by the guards. After getting back on the road they had a mile and a half hike to the highway.

"How are we going to work this?" asked Carol. "It is thirty miles to the nearest town, and we have no money."

"The state patrol comes along here periodically," answered George. "But how can we explain a cluster of six people on the side of the road."

"The next town is Barstow," said Carl. "It just so happens that I have a valid bank card in my wallet.

There is no reason why it shouldn't be valid after 10 yeas. Suppose Nancy and I stand up by the road and the rest of you stay back here. When the state patrol comes along, I'll show him my bank card and talk him into taking Nancy and me to Barstow. Then I'll use my bank card to get some money. I will hire a taxi and come back here to get the rest of you."

After some discussion, that was agreed to. When the state patrol came along about 45 minutes later, Nancy and Carl flagged him down. The officer decided to drive them to Barstow after seeing Carl's bankcard. The officer was able to use his radio to call in to the state patrol station and ascertain that the bank card was valid.

Carl hired a taxi and was back at the intersection of the side road with the highway in a little over an hour. Nancy soon arrived in a second taxi. They picked up the other four group members and headed for Barstow.

When they were all comfortably ensconced at a motel and sitting in the motel restaurant, Carl said, "I didn't have any trouble at all using my bank card at the motel. The card and bank account are perfectly valid even if they haven't been used in ten years."

# Chapter 15

Everyone went to breakfast at the motel restaurant at 9 am the next morning. When the waitress came, they all placed their orders. The waitress brought coffee immediately.

Nancy's first remark was, "I am going to telephone my parents today. I just don't know what to say about where I have been the last ten years."

Carl said, "We want to make sure everybody is back safely before we start talking about where we have been."

"But that will take a month and a half or two months," said Janet.

"Yes," answered Carl. "But we can't put the others in jeopardy. There are still over ninety people on Titan."

"Well what can we say to people down here for the next couple of months?" asked Gayle.

"How would it be if we said something like 'I can't say anything now because it might jeopardize the safety of some other people'?" asked Nancy.

Gayle said, "The first thing they are going to ask is 'What do you mean by safe? Not safe in what way?'"

"You can say that you can't reveal that," answered Nancy.

"You know that if you are talking to your parents, they are going to say that you should go to the police and get police help," said George.

"Well then you can ask them to wait 45 days," responded Nancy.

"I think your parents will be afraid you and your friends are in very deep trouble and should call the police immediately," said Carl.

"I think there is a missing person police file document already on file for most of us," said George.

"I think you're right," said Janet. "Probably eighty out of the hundred of us have missing person documents on file."

"Yes, but there might be a thousand of those things filed every year in America," said George.

"Most of us never knew each other before we became caught up in this," said Gayle. "I don't think the police will link us all up."

"But all one hundred of us—whether we knew each other or not—had occasion to be around Barstow, California before we became missing persons," said Carl.

"If one of us were to come to the attention of the police now, there would be an investigation," said George.

"I imagine any one at all, from any State, who was on a missing persons list is going to be investigated by the police," said George.

"It just occurred to me," said Carl, "that when I used my bank card last night I might have started something."

"How?" asked Nancy.

"Well, maybe the police watch bank cards and credit cards of anyone on the missing persons list," said Carl.

"Well, it's too late now to change your actions," said Janet. "Besides, you had to use your card. The rest of us were all standing out on that road last night."

"We have to devise a sensible way to deal with this issue," said George. "We can't just wait until everybody is back safely. What if it takes a year? We're just thinking it will take a month and a half or two months."

"What if we wait two months before telling our story?" asked Gayle. "Maybe telling our story at that point will help those people, if any, who are still stuck there."

Everybody was quiet for a while, thinking the thing over.

"What are the Pros and Cons of telling our story?" asked Carol. "If we do tell it, then the Philadelphians will find out about it immediately. A police investigation down here will become known to them immediately."

"And then a careful hunt will be instituted up there on Titan," responded Janet, "and those remaining up there won't be able to stow away on a shuttle ship to come down here."

"On the other hand," continued Carol, "if we don't tell our story right now then there will not be a police investigation right now. That would give the people still up there on Titan a chance to get back to earth. Maybe it will take a year, two months might be optimistic."

"I don't think we should remain silent too long," said George. "This situation might have been going on for fifteen years already."

"I think that to give the people we know about up there a reasonable chance, we should wait six months," said Carl. "After that, we should tell our story. This situation shouldn't be allowed to go on indefinitely."

"Does anyone want to extend it to ten months?" asked George.

"I move for a compromise," said Gayle. "I suggest eight months."

"I second the motion for eight months," said Janet.

"Any discussion?" asked George.

No response.

"All in favor say aye," chimed George.

Everyone said aye.

"Moved and passed for eight months," said George.

"So, what do we say to our parents, now?" asked Nancy. "Should we just say nothing?"

"Suppose a person writes a letter to a family member," said Carl, "and says he or she is all right and back in Los Angeles, but doesn't want to talk about it for a while. Do not put a return address on the envelope."

"That ought to work fine," responded George. "If the letter is postmarked and mailed in Los Angeles, the recipient will treat it as genuine."

"OK," said Nancy. "I'll do that."

"I don't think I'll use my bank card again," said Carl. "The police might track the usage of a bank card belonging to a missing person."

"So, should we all go to Los Angeles and look for jobs?" asked Nancy.

"If you apply for a job, you will have to use your name," answered Gayle, "and you might be on a missing persons list."

"I have quite a bit of cash, over 100 thousand, in a bank deposit drawer," said George. "I sold a house and was looking for another house when I got caught up in this space thing. The bank deposit drawer is under my brother's name. He moved to Europe to take a job and just gave me the bank deposit drawer and key. My brother maintains the bank account because he has a savings account at the bank."

"That would be great," said Carl. "Just put a little book in the deposit drawer and record how much you loan to each of us over the next eight months."

"Yes, applying for a job might lead to difficulties for the next eight months," said Gayle.

They left the restaurant and went to their rooms. It was a nice day out as usual and so they went for a walk.

A few went to the shopping mall, some to a book store, others just set out on a pleasant stroll.

Nancy and Carl went for a walk down the main downtown street.

Nancy said, "I have always heard that rent is very high in Los Angeles."

"So have I," answered Carl. "But it can't be high all over or there wouldn't be over eight million people living there."

"They also have gangs and drugs," persisted Nancy.

"We could pick another town," said Carl.

"If it is very pleasant, then it will be very expensive," continued Nancy.

"How abort Oxnard or Riverside," said Carl. "I don't want to get too far away from Barstow because I have to drive up there every Thursday and Sunday to see if any of our people arrived."

"Riverside would probably be all right," said Nancy, "if the smog isn't too bad."

"We could rent five or six apartments for the six of us," said Nancy.

"We will probably want to buy a second hand car," said Carl, "for shopping and other errands."

"You could use it every Thursday and Sunday to go to Barstow," said Nancy.

"Yes," said Carl. "According to Colonel Smith's records over the past months, a shuttle leaves Titan every Tuesday and arrives on earth every Thursday and another shuttle leaves Titan every Friday and arrives on earth every Sunday."

"We will need more than six apartments pretty quick," said Nancy.

"Yes, I don't know how we are going to work this," said Carl. "You need a social security card to get a job."

"We will need a town with a lot of cheap apartments," continued Carl.

"What if we rented old houses, instead of apartments?" asked Nancy.

"We will have to check all this out on the Internet," said Carl. "We can try different cities."

"This is going to be a real discipline for eight months," said Nancy. "All this stuff to buy and we don't have much money to use."

"We better get out of our current motel rooms today," said Carl, "since I used my bank card to pay. It won't take long before police departments with missing person lists will spot the use of my bank card."

When they got back to the motel, the others were there.

Carl said, "To repeat again what I said earlier, I paid the motel fee using my bank card and that transaction record will probably reach the missing persons bureau soon. So, we better check out right after lunch."

Everybody agreed. The lunch special in the restaurant was baked lasagna. Several of the six ordered it and said that it was very good.

"Is your bank deposit drawer in Los Angeles, George?" asked Carl.

"Yes," answered George. "It's in Pasadena."

"Then we all better take the Greyhound bus to Pasadena this afternoon," said Carl. "I still have enough money for that without using my bank card again.

After lunch they walked to the bus depot. The bus left Barstow at 1 pm and arrived in Pasadena at 5 pm.

During the ride, Carl told George of the conversation he had had with Nancy about living quarters.

"I know of several old but adequate houses we could rent," said George.

"You are right," continued George, "accommodations for one hundred people could be expensive."

"Of course," said Carl, "the hundred people could all be here in two months as we anticipate. So, we won't need to rent for eight months."

"That's true," said George.

"It might be interesting to check on our old belongings," said Carl. "I suppose most of that was sent to our relatives."

"Probably," said George. "Usually on an apartment form there is a space for a person to notify in an emergency."

"I wonder if any of the hundred people was important enough, socially, to get mentioned in the newspaper when they disappeared," said Carl.

"Well, Colonel Smith might have been important," suggested George. "That's a pretty high military rank."

"Yes," said Carl.

"Do you know if any of the hundred had a relative who was a politician or the chief executive officer of a highly visible company like a bank or department store?" asked Carl.

"Well my father owns a chain of four restaurants," said George.

"Then you could check the Los Angeles Times for the week of your disappearance," said Carl.

"I intend to," said George.

"Does that newspaper keep a computer file of their main articles on their web site?" asked Carl.

"I think so," said George, "and the records would go back at least ten years."

"In any case, you could probably go into their office and view records of back issues," said Carl.

After the rest stop, Carl sat with Nancy and George with Carol.

"There is no rush, but we could start thinking about what we are going to say in our report of what happened to us," said Nancy.

"Yes," said Carl, "and to whom we are going to say it."

"We could write it up," said Nancy. "Everybody could contribute."

"There would be a lot of really interesting stuff in there about those space ships and traveling near the speed of light," said Carl.

"The young generation would be fascinated," said Nancy. "Think of sleeping for four years while you travel at nine tenths the speed of light."

"Wow, big time," said Carl with a grin, "if you are eight or nine years old."

When they got to the bus depot in Pasadena, George said, "Why don't you people stay here. I'll take a taxi over to my bank and get some money. I think it is open till six."

They all agreed and George left in a hurry. The others went into the Greyhound cafeteria and got a doughnut and something to drink.

About an hour later, George returned with a grin on his face. "I've got it," he said. "I took out a few hundred for now. I have had my car key, house key, and bank deposit key on my key chain for way over ten years."

"Of course, your car and house are gone now," said Carol, "but you still have the bank key."

Carl said, "George, here is a note book that I bought on Titan using my salary as a warehouse worker. You can keep track of the loans you make to each of us."

"Thank you, Carl," said George, "I will treat it as a souvenir from Titan and also use it as a business record."

"It is almost 7 pm," said George. "Let's find a few hotel rooms for tonight. Tomorrow, we can buy a serviceable second hand car and start a serious search for living accommodations."

They found an old fashioned hotel downtown. The halls were wide, the ceilings were high, and there were rugs on the wooden floor.

"Boy, this must be an old building," said Carl.

"The ceilings are ten feet high," said Nancy. "I guess that lets the hot air rise up high and keeps it cool below."

"Maybe this place is some kind of a period piece from the past that they are maintaining for today," said Carl.

"It looks very nicely maintained," said Nancy. "I hope they have air conditioners and modern plumbing."

They all went out to supper that night. They found an elegant restaurant with grand chandeliers and leaded windows. The menu was six pages long and had lots of French words and no pictures. The waitresses wore dresses, not pants suits, of eighteenth century European design. Carl had roast lamb and Nancy chose roast duck. After dinner they all sat in the lounge room and had coffee or a drink.

George said, "It has been suggested that we look for lodgings in Oxnard or Riverside. Those are both OK. Ventura would also be fine."

Nancy said, "The main thing for now is that we stay along the main highway to Barstow. Carl has to drive there every Thursday and Sunday."

"Another consideration is that we might want to rent several old houses once our group gets up to eighty or a hundred people," said George. "Nancy suggested that to Carl, earlier."

"You can rent computers at the desk in our hotel to look things up on the Internet," said Gayle.

"Good idea," said Carl. "I'll rent one and spend some time looking for house rentals on the Internet. I know the whole general area fairly well."

"I will go out early tomorrow morning," said George, "and try to find a second hand car. What do you think of a van? We might all be able to cram into it."

"I have been thinking about the car situation," said Carl. "To drive the car you need a driver's license and to get a driver's license you have to identify yourself. As soon as you give them your name, they will look up your name and discover you are listed as a missing person. I think we had better use the bus and taxies for now and get a car latter after we have told our story."

Everybody reluctantly agreed. They were all looking forward to having a car.

With that, they returned to their hotel. Carl got a computer at the front desk and took it up to his room. It was still early so several of the others came in and crowded around. They started looking for house rentals.

"Here are some houses in Riverside for rent," said Carl. "They are listed with pictures."

"There's a four bedroom house for $2000 per month," said Janet. "The picture doesn't look too bad."

"We are not going to be living there for very long. At most eight months," said Gayle.

"Here's another one," said Carl. "Four bedrooms for $2400 pet month. Also, the house looks fine in the picture."

"It would certainly be nice if we could buy a car to use," said George, "but then one of us would have to get a driver's license."

"And that would mean that one of us would have to reveal his identity," said Carl, "and we don't want to do that for eight months."

"I guess we will just have to be content with the bus system," said Gayle.

Carl then switched to newspapers. He clicked on the Los Angeles Times and got their web page.

"What should we enter into the search box?" Carl asked.

"Try missing person and 2125," said Gayle.

They got a number of records with missing person highlighted and a bunch of records with 2125 highlighted.

"Do you recognize any names?" asked Carl.

"Not yet," answered Gayle.

After going through several pages, George said, "There I am!"

Carl selected the record and got the half column article on George's disappearance.

"It says here," said Carl. "'George Erickson has been missing for twenty days. Mr. Erickson makes monthly business trips to Barstow and Las Vegas. Mr. Erickson is the son of Charles Erickson, owner of the Erickson Restaurant chain in Los Angeles.' It goes on to say a few things about your brother and sister. It says 'George Erickson has a brother, Ralph, living in Rotterdam, Holland.'"

"I'll go back to the main search engine and try missing person and 2125 again," said Carl.

They got ten pages of references again.

"Do you see Ralph Smith on any of these pages?" asked Carl.

"He might not have been from Los Angeles," said Janet. "Maybe he was just stationed around here somewhere."

"Go back to the top of the search engine and type US Army Ralph Smith into the search box," said Nancy.

Carl did that and the computer came up with a page of three or four references. Carl high lighted one with his mouse and said, "Here is one that might have what we want."

When the page came onto the screen, Carl read, "A Fort Adams public relations bulletin states 'Army Colonel Ralph Smith has not reported to his duty station in ten days. His wife, Denise, says that she has had no contact with her husband. Colonel Smith was on temporary assignment in California.' "

"So, at least two of us have been reported as missing," said Nancy.

The next morning Carl and Nancy checked the Internet for house rentals again.

"Let's write down some of these addresses and prices," said Nancy.

Nancy's first choice was a house at 12405 Summer Ave W in Riverside at $2400 per month. The real estate phone number was listed and Carl wrote it down. After 45 minutes they had ten addresses in the vicinity of Riverside. Carl telephoned the real estate agency in each case to find out if the house was still available. Half an hour later they had confirmation that seven of the houses were still available.

By 11 am Nancy and Cal had completed their task. They found the others in the television and recreation room of the hotel.

"We have a list of seven houses for rent in Riverside," said Nancy. "Carl and I telephoned about each one and they are still available."

"They're all about $2400 per month," said Carl. "We could check out of our hotel at noon and take the bus down to Riverside to view the houses."

"Good idea," said George.

They checked out of their rooms and had lunch in the hotel restaurant. Then all six got onto a bus and headed to Riverside. They visited the seven houses and by 4 o'clock they had selected three houses that didn't require leases.

"We still have time to buy some furniture at a second hand furniture store," said Janet.

By seven o'clock they had out fitted the bedrooms, kitchens, and living rooms of their three homes. The homes were less than a mile apart from each other.

"We will get telephones installed tomorrow," said George, "and then we will be settled for awhile."

That evening Carl said to the others, "I have been thinking about how I can meet the next groups on Thursday and Sunday evenings. For example, to meet the group arriving on Sunday, I'll take the bus from Riverside to Barstow on Sunday morning. Then Sunday afternoon I'll take a taxi cab from Barstow to the intersection of the highway with that road to the space ship landing field. I'll arrange with the taxi cab to come back to the same spot at 6 pm. Then I'll walk to the base and wait for the next group of our people to get off the space shuttle."

"That's a long arduous weekend," said Janet.

"Yes, a car would make it easier," said Carl, "but we had better not try to get a driver's license at this time."

"We should be back at Riverside by midnight from Barstow," said Carl. "I checked the bus schedule."

"Let's hope this whole process doesn't take more than two months," said George. "Maybe we could take turns going out to Barstow on Thursdays and Sundays."

Everything went smoothly and in just seven weeks all one hundred Californians had returned safely to Riverside from Titan. They had to rent more houses as the weeks went by and at the end of the seven weeks they had ten houses altogether.

"Now that we are all back," said Carl one Friday evening, "it is time to put our plan in motion."

Each of the ten houses sent a representative to Carl's house for a meeting every Friday night.

"Various approaches have been proposed," said Carl, "and evaluated. It is pretty much agreed that our government has been trying to conceal this involvement with Titan where we supply them with supplies and equipment. Our government can't do anything else since we are militarily inferior to Titan. Rather than admit our inferiority to the people, our government has chosen to conceal the activity. Maybe our government has chosen the best solution. If our government had refused to aid the Philadelphians, the Philadelphians might have taken over the country."

"So, it won't achieve anything to report all this to a government agency," put in Janet.

"I think our best bet is to tell our story to two or three newspapers simultaneously," said Carl.

"We could prepare our story, write it up, and send one of us with a copy of the story to each of those newspapers on the same day," said George.

"What if they don't print it?" asked one of the representatives in attendance.

"We can't control that," answered Nancy. "We can only present our story."

"Do you think it would help to present our story to a TV station as well?" asked another representative.

"It might," replied Carl.

"The main thing, I think," said Carl, "is to write the story as an informative document, not a call to action."

"I agree," said George. "A call to action will meet with resistance."

"So, the story is just going to inform the public of what is going on?" asked someone.

"Yes, pretty much," answered Carl.

"So, which newspapers have you chosen?" asked a representative.

"We were thinking of the Los Angeles Times, the New York Times, and the London Times," said George.

"How about telling our story to some news caster on a TV station?" asked Janet.

"Isn't everything they say very carefully checked by executives before they say it?" asked Gayle.

"Probably," answered Carl.

"I think I can arrange an interview at the Los Angles Times," said George. "I know some one there."

"I can do the same at the New York Times and London Times," said Colonel Smith.

"I nominate George to go to the Los Angeles Times, Carl to go to the New York Times, and Colonel Smith to go to the London Times," said Gayle.

"I second the motion," said Janet.

"Any discussion?" asked Carl.

"Could we go back to our houses and present the nominations?" asked a representative.

"Certainly," said Carl. "Take a vote on the nominations and bring the vote record here next Friday."

The meeting then turned to the substance of the newspaper reports. After two hours of discussion the representatives returned to their homes.

The following Friday, a representative from each house came to Carl's house. The votes from all ten houses showed agreement with Carl and George's plan. A committee from the ten houses to formulate the document was established. The committee met daily for a week and formulated the document. George and Colonel Smith telephoned their long standing contacts within the three newspapers. A meeting was arranged at each newspaper for November 15.

# Chapter 16

Carl flew to New York on November 14th.

At 9 am on November 15th, Carl was ushered into the office of Richard Adams, a New York Times columnist.

Richard Adams stood and came around his desk to shake hands with Carl. "Good morning, Mr. Carl Johnson, I am pleased to meet you."

Carl answered, "Good morning, Mr. Adams, it is a pleasure to meet you."

"Please have a seat, Mr. Johnson. May I call you Carl?" Richard Adams gestured towards a chair.

"Yes, of course," answered Carl.

It was a medium size office with a window giving a view of New York City. Richard Adams was about 40 years of age, had brown curly hair, and had brown eyes. He wore a nicely tailored blue suit, a white shirt, and a conservative red tie. Richard Adams sat down behind a large mahogany desk. A picture of a scene along the Hudson River adorned one of the light blue walls.

"Colonel Ralph Smith telephoned me," began Richard Adams, "to tell me that you were a former missing person. I've known Ralph Smith for many years. We were class mates at Columbia."

"Yes, I left the country about ten years ago," replied Carl, "and returned recently. Since I was unable to contact anyone here, I suppose I was declared a missing person."

"You were held incommunicado someplace?" asked Richard Adams.

"Actually, I was off the planet for ten years," answered Carl.

Richard Adam's eye brows rose slightly. Carl wondered if Richard Adams might think him a psychiatric case

"Off the planet, you say?" asked Richard Adams.

"Yes, it is the story that I have come to tell you about," answered Carl. "Your friend, Colonel Ralph Smith, was also a missing person for ten years. Our paths crossed during that time period."

"I was a computer programmer in the Los Angeles area about ten years ago," began Carl. "The company I worked for sent me to a military base in the California desert about once a month and I passed Barstow on the way."

"Can you tell me the name of the company?" asked Richard Adams.'

"It was General Engineering Company," replied Carl, "and the base I went to was near Canyon City, California. Actually, I had two ways to get to the base. I could turn from highway 15 directly onto highway 395 and go to the base or I could go through Barstow and then go over to highway 395 and from there go to the base."

Richard Adams wrote the information down on a pad and looked back up at Carl.

"I have this complete story written up in this folder," said Carl, waving a gray folder.

"I just wanted to say it first."

"Certainly," responded Richard Adams.

"One night, about ten years ago," continued Carl, "I noticed what looked like a spaceship land out in the desert."

Again Richard Adams looked intently at Carl.

Carl thought Richard Adams was appraising him again.

"I continued on my way to the military base," said Carl. "I told a fellow worker of mine at the base what I had seen. Her name is Nancy Jones. She might have thought I was crazy, but she was interested nevertheless. We agreed to stop at the area along the highway on a future trip. The next month, we did. When we parked the car and walked to the area in the desert, we saw a spaceship parked on a landing pad."

Carl shifted his weight in the chair and crossed his legs. He continued, "We were nosey and went up into the spaceship. The door was open."

Richard Adams asked, "What is this lady's name again?"

Carl answered, "Nancy Jones. She has also been listed as a missing person these last ten years."

Richard Adams wrote this down and returned his gaze to Carl. He touched his pen to his lips as he considered Carl.

Carl continued, "While we were on board the spaceship, the spaceship suddenly closed its doors and lifted off. I am quite sure they didn't know we were aboard. The spaceship flew to the Titan moon of the planet Saturn. There is a large colony of former colonists from earth on Titan. They are called Philadelphians. They look exactly like us since they originally came from several European countries and the United States. They left as colonists on spaceships about a hundred and thirty five years ago to establish a colony on a planet in the Alpha Centauri star system. I have some photographs of them in this folder which I will leave with you. In fact, I can show you one now."

Carl reached into his folder and pulled out a photograph. He handed it to Richard Adams. Richard Adams studied the photograph carefully.

Richard Adams handed back the photograph and asked, "You say there are a large number of these people on the moon, Titan?"

"Yes, several thousand," answered Carl.

"How come the rest of us have never seen them?" asked Richard Adams.

"That is actually pretty much the reason I came here to tell you my story," answered Carl. "You see these people are very highly advanced. Much more advanced technologically than us. The colonists who left earth a hundred and thirty five years ago established separate nations on their planet in Alpha Centauri. They got into a nuclear war on their planet in the Alpha Centauri sun system and one nation was defeated. That nation, called New Philadelphia, can no longer live on their planet because their region is contaminated by radio activity. So, they decided to come back to our solar system. They landed here but decided they didn't want to stay. They only want to use our industrial complex to outfit themselves with a new military armada. Then they will go back to their region in Alpha Centauri and establish another domain."

"But you said we are far behind them," interrupted Richard Adams.

"That is true," said Carl. "We are merely supplying the natural resources. They have their own factories on Titan and are constructing highly advanced spaceships there. I'll give you a picture of one of their spaceships."

Carl again reached into his folder and selected a photograph of a Philadelphian spaceship. He passed it to Richard Adams.

Richard Adams accepted the photograph and studied it intently. He hunched forward and examined it with enormous interest.

Carl said, "That spaceship is 400 feet long and can fly at nine tenths the speed of light."

Richard Adams looked up from the photograph and just stared at Carl.

After a moment, Richard Adams said, "Would it be all right if I lent this photograph and the other photograph of the man to one of our technicians for an hour? I would like to have him examine the photograph."

"Yes," said Carl. "That would be all right."

He reached back into his folder and retrieved the other photograph. He handed it across the desk to Richard Adams.

"What kind of camera did you use?" asked Richard Adams.

"It was just one of the digital cameras made in America. The Certa brand, I think. America runs a space shuttle system to Titan and supplies them with what ever they need or want."

Richard Adams picked up his phone and dialed a number. After a minute he spoke, "Hans, could you come up here a minute."

Richard Adams said, "Did you say that America operates a shuttle system and supplies their needs?"

"Yes," answered Carl. "Here is the conjectural part of the story. We are of the opinion that the American government realized that we are no match militarily for the Philadelphians. So, our government entered into an agreement with the Philadelphians whereby we supply the resources they need for constructing spaceships if they leave our solar system after they complete the building of their military armada."

"Why is our government keeping this such a secret?" asked Richard Adams.

"Well, we are of the opinion," answered Carl, "that our government is afraid to admit to the people that it is incapable of defending America against an alien foe."

"That sounds a little preposterous," responded Richard Adams.

"Yes, it does," concede Carl, "but it seems to fit."

"So, why were you gone ten years?" asked Richard Adams.

At that moment, Hans entered the room and asked, "What is it that you need?"

Richard Adams handed him the two photographs. "Examine these, please, for authenticity, etcetera. They were taken with a Certa camera."

Hans took the photographs and left.

"Where were we?" asked Richard. "Oh, yes, why were you gone ten years?"

Carl answered, "We were captured on Titan. Actually, they had accumulated one hundred prisoners over the years. When they completed their armada, they set out for Alpha Centauri to regain a living space. They took us along as prisoners."

"Alpha Centauri?" asked Richard Adams.

"Yes," answered Carl. "It is a star system about four light years from here. They took us along as prisoners. When we arrived there, the Philadelphians had a battle with the Dynasty and lost."

"The Dynasty?" asked Richard Adams.

"Yes," answered Carl. "The Dynasty is composed of the earth colonists and rules the region about Alpha Centauri. They are the offspring of the 600 colonists who left here in the year 2000; they refer to themselves as the New Barstonians. Anyway, the Dynasty defeated the Philadelphians; or I should say, the Dynasty drove the Philadelphians away. However, the Dynasty captured us."

"So, where did the defeated Philadelphians go?" asked Richard Adams.

"Back to Titan, as best we can tell," answered Carl.

"All hundred of us prisoners escaped the Dynasty after a year, and came back to Titan," continued Carl. "We refurbished a spaceship that was in the Dynasty junk yard."

"That must have been quite an undertaking," said Richard Adams. "You said their technology is way advanced over ours."

"Yes," responded Carl, "but they had blueprints and they had worked out the technology. All we had to do was use their technology."

Richard Adams sat looking at Carl and wondering if this story was true.

"It has always been my contention," said Carl, "that it takes very smart people a very long time to develop a technology. But after the technology is developed, a smart person, not necessarily a genius, can learn the technology quite rapidly. For example, modern mathematics and physics took centuries to develop. And, it took geniuses to develop it. However, today any ordinary smart person can learn it in a four year college program."

At that point Hans came back in the room and handed Richard Adams the photographs and a sheet of paper. Richard Adams read the paper and said, "Our laboratory has determined that the photographs are genuine and have not been modified or altered."

"So, how did you get back to earth?" asked Richard Adams.

"After we returned to Titan from Alpha Centauri," said Carl, "we developed a scheme whereby we stowed away aboard the Titan to Earth shuttles. It took us almost two months since only eight or ten at a time could come."

"So, are there a hundred of you now in California?" asked Richard Adams.

"Yes," answered Carl. "We are living in ten houses in Riverside, California. We are now bringing our story out, and want to re-enter normal life. We will contact our families, get jobs, and get drivers licenses."

"Why did you choose a newspaper to tell your story?" asked Richard Adams.

"We thought the government would try to suppress it," answered Carl, "if we chose some other way to bring out the story."

"We just think the people ought to know about it," said Carl. "We are not trying to give the government a hard time. We just think the government is wrong in thinking the people will panic if they hear their government can not protect them from an external power. I think the people can stand up to that knowledge; they won't panic or fall apart."

"So you want us to print your story," said Richard Adams.

"Yes," answered Carl.

"Well, I will have to read the report you have in your folder and conduct interviews with the hundred people in Riverside. Are their addresses in your folder?"

"Yes," answered Carl. "By the way, you will find two small figurines in plastic bags attached to the folder. We obtained one of them at the Dynasty base in Alpha Centauri and the other on Titan. You can have them chemically analyzed."

Richard Adams rose from his desk and accepted the folder. He said, "I will read your report and arrange interviews with the hundred people in Riverside. Thank you very much for your visit, Carl Johnson."

They shook hands and Carl left.

# Chapter 17

When Carl got back to Riverside, California, Nancy asked, "How did it go?"

Carl answered, "The interview at the New York Times went well. They seemed impressed by the photographs."

Nancy asked, "Are they going to publish our report?"

Carl answered, "They are going to come out here to interview all of us. They want to interview us before they publish the story."

George Erickson returned to Riverside, California from Los Angeles the following day. He stopped by the house where Carl was living that evening. The residents of the house sat in the living room and listened to George's account of his interview with the Los Angeles Times newspaper.

"What was the name of the reporter you spoke to?" asked Nancy.

"Her name was Helen Alexander," answered George. "I met her years ago when I was working at my father's company and we sponsored something of public interest at the time."

"Was she receptive of our plan?" asked Gayle.

"Yes," answered George. "I think they might publish our report."

"She must have been totally amazed by our experience," said Janet.

"Yes, for sure," said George.

"When you told her that there were a hundred others, did she say she was going to start checking the missing person files for them?" asked Gayle.

"Yes," said George.

"I suppose newspaper reporters are good at checking public files and documents," said Gayle.

"The photographs really impressed her," said George.

"Yes," responded Carl. "The person I spoke to at the New York Times took a great interest in them."

"Helen Alexander asked me if one of the newspaper technicians could examine the pictures," said George.

"That's what happened with me, also," said Carl.

"The technician returned about an hour later," said George, "and said the pictures were authentic."

"Did you tell Helen that we were meeting with the New York Times and London Times?" asked Carl.

"Yes," answered George.

"The New York Times is going to send some reporter out here to Riverside, California to interview all of us," said Carl.

George said, "The Los Angeles Times will do the same."

Several days later, Colonel Smith returned to Riverside, California from London. The next day he went to Carl's house to report on his interview with the London Times.

"Who was the person you spoke to at the London Times?" asked George.

"His name is Denis Miller," said Colonel Smith. "I had met him years ago. I had been stationed for a while in England and Denis Miller was a British army officer at the time."

"Did the interview go well?" asked Nancy.

"Yes, it did," answered Colonel Smith.

"Do you think they will publish our document?" asked Carl.

"They plan on coming here to interview us first," said Colonel Smith.

"So, we will have reporters from the London Times, New York Times, and Los Angeles Times," said Carol.

"Yes, they are all interested," said Carl.

"I showed our photographs and little figurines to Denis Miller," said Colonel Smith.

"One of their technicians verified the authenticity of the photographs while I was there," continued Colonel Smith.

"The same thing occurred with Carl and me," said George.

"I had to stay a few days in London," said Colonel Smith, "due to airline flight reservations. So, Denis Miller telephoned me at my hotel to tell me that the report on the little figurines came back from the laboratory. They were really impressed by the results."

"In what way were they impressed?" asked Nancy.

"Well, they did a chemical analysis on the material used in the figurines," said Colonel Smith. "They said they think the material is not used on earth to manufacture anything."

"Is it a different type of material?" asked Gayle.

"No," answered Colonel Smith. "The material has to be composed of the same elements that are present on the earth. The number of elements is the same all over the universe. It was the particular alloy or mixture of the elements that was unique."

"I suppose if someone made a figurine out of the material of a meteor, that struck the earth, that would be a unique figurine," said Nancy.

"Yes," said Colonel Smith.

The interviews began the following week in Riverside. There were reporters from the London Times, New York Times, and Los Angeles Times in attendance.

The newspapers had spent several days gathering missing person records from police and public institutions in the California area. They requested records that covered the past ten years. The newspapers then compared the names of the hundred people mentioned in Carl's report with the missing persons records. They found matches with many of the hundred people.

One day during the interview process, Richard Adams interviewed Gayle Poitiers.

"Good morning, Gayle Poitiers, my name is Richard Adams. I am a reporter for the New York Times."

"Good morning," said Gayle.

"I understand you were a nurse in California ten years ago," said Richard Adams.

"Yes," answered Gayle.

"How did you manage to get caught up in all this?" asked Richard Adams.

"Oh, my friend, Janet Snyder, and I were driving on highway 395 about thirty miles from Barstow, California one night ten years ago," said Gayle, "and we saw a flying saucer land. We were returning to Los Angeles from a medical meeting at a hospital in Barstow."

"And, you went to investigate?" asked Richard Adams.

"Yes," answered Gayle.

"Well, were you captured?" asked Richard Adams.

"No, at least not at first," answered Gayle.

"What happened?" asked Richard Adams.

"We drove over to the spaceship," answered Gayle, "and got out of our car. We walked over to the spaceship and saw that one of its doors was open."

"And out of curiosity, you had to go in the open door?" asked Richard Adams.

"Yes," answered Gayle. "But I will never let curiosity get the better of me again."

"According to Carl Johnson's report," said Richard Adams, "you people went on a four year trip and you slept for the whole four years."

"Yes," replied Gayle, "it was a dreadful experience."

"In what way?" asked Richard Adams.

"Well, it is terrifying," answered Gayle. "You are going to sleep for four years. How do you know if you'll ever wake up?"

"Yes, indeed," answered Richard Adams.

"Or, how do you know you will be the same when you wake up?" asked Gayle.

"I don't suppose you had a choice," said Richard Adams. "Were you just told that you had to cooperate in this four year sleep?"

"Well, we were told that there is not enough food or water for a person to stay awake for four years," said Gayle. "Your only chance for survival is to go into this long sleep."

"Well, what does this bed or sleeping capsule look like?" asked Richard Adams.

"It is a small completely enclosed bed with a cover," said Gayle.

"So, were there a hundred of these things on the spaceship?" asked Richard Adams.

"Yes," answered Gayle. "At a certain time on a certain day, everyone is told to get into his sleeping capsule and close the glass lid. Then you press a button and music starts and a gas is introduced into the capsule and you fall asleep."

Denis Miller of the London Times interviewed Carl on the third day of the interviews.

"Good morning, Carl Johnson, my name is Denis Miller. I am a reporter from the London Times."

"Good morning," said Carl.

"This is certainly an extraordinary experience for all of us," began Denis Miller.

"Yes, it is," responded Carl.

"First, we reporters have to determine that this is not just a hoax," said Denis Miller.

"Yes, you are bound to wonder about that," said Carl.

"We at the London Times were very impressed by the photographs and the little figurines or statues," said Denis Miller.

"Oh, right," responded Carl.

"Our technicians determined that the photographs were genuine," said Denis Miller. "They said they could easily determine that they were taken by a Certa digital camera, a brand made in America. But the important thing was that the photographs were not modified after they were taken."

"Yes, that would be something to check," said Carl.

"And, the figurines were chemically analyzed," said Denis Miller. "The substance they were made of was very unusual. The substance was a combination of the standard elements, of course. It would have to be that way. The same elements are found all over the universe."

"Was it the combination of the standard elements, that went into the alloy, that was unusual?" asked Carl.

"Yes, it was an unusual combination or mixture that the metal workers used when they made the metal," said Denis Miller.

Helen Alexander of the Los Angeles Times interviewed Colonel Smith on the fifth day of interviews.

"Good morning, Colonel Smith, my name is Helen Alexander. I am a reporter with the Los Angeles Times."

"Good morning, Helen Alexander," said Colonel Smith.

"This whole thing seems to have been carried on like a secret operation," said Helen Alexander.

"Yes, it seems that way," said Colonel Smith.

"According to Carl Johnson's report," said Helen Alexander, "a space shuttle system has been running between earth and the Titan moon of Saturn for some time."

"Yes, that is the way it appears," said Colonel Smith.

"Well, how many shuttle trips are made per month, Colonel?" asked Helen Alexander.

"We counted them for a while when we were still on Titan," said Colonel Smith. "We wanted to figure out a way to get all one hundred of us back to earth. We counted about two shuttle trips per week."

"Two shuttle trips per week," said Helen Alexander. "And how big was the payload of a shuttle?"

"Well, we couldn't determine that for sure," said Colonel Smith.

"How big is one of those shuttles?" asked Helen Alexander.

"They are about 500 feet long and about 300 feet wide," answered Colonel Smith.

"I wonder how many tons of cargo could fit in that," said Helen Alexander.

"I don't think the cargo is a very heavy material," said Colonel Smith. "We don't think they carried heavy material like steel."

"What was it then?" asked Helen Alexander.

"Perhaps an alloy of aluminum," answered Colonel Smith.

"Do you know what the people on Titan used the materials for?" asked Helen Alexander.

"We think they used the material of our natural resources to make spaceships," answered Colonel Smith.

"How many spaceships do you think they have constructed?" asked Helen Alexander.

"We don't know for sure," answered Colonel Smith "but we were taken along as prisoners on one of their military armadas. There must have been at least 50 spaceships in that armada."

"How big is that base on Titan?" asked Helen Alexander.

"It is probably about three quarters of a mile long and half a mile wide," answered Colonel Smith.

"How many people are there?" asked Helen Alexander.

"There must be several thousand," answered Colonel Smith.

"What do you think, Colonel Smith, will happen if we publish this document?" asked Helen Alexander.

"Well, the first thing that will probably happen," said Colonel Smith, "is that a lot of people will drive up to Barstow and try to see the base and spaceships."

"No doubt," responded Helen Alexander.

"Of course, they can be kept off the base," said Colonel Smith, "because it is a military base."

"Do you think the spaceships will continue to land there if the report is printed in the newspapers?" asked Helen.

"I imagine they will use another base somewhere," said Colonel Smith.

"What do you suppose our government will say when the article is published?" asked Helen Alexander.

"That is hard to say," answered Colonel Smith.

"Your theory is that our government is accommodating these Titan people because we are so far behind them technologically that we can't refuse their demands. That is your theory isn't it?" asked Helen Alexander.

"That is our theory, yes," answered Colonel Smith.

"So, our government might not respond to the newspaper article," said Helen Alexander. "It might just move the operation to another location."

"Yes, that could happen," said Colonel Smith.

"Or, they might respond to the newspaper report. They might admit what is going on," said Helen Alexander.

Two weeks later a front page article appeared in all three newspapers describing the ten year ordeal of the hundred people.

The United States government responded to the articles by stating that when the Philadelphians first made their demands for manufactured goods twenty years ago, the United States government conferred with all of our allies. Every government agreed that we would have to accommodate the Philadelphians since we could not defy them; the Philadelphians were too far ahead of us in technology. The United States government decided to not inform the public of the situation since the government felt that a lot of people would be overly anxious if they thought their government could not protect them from people from outer space.